SONG OF PLANET EARTH

LEIGHTON K. CHONG

authorHOUSE®

AuthorHouse™
1663 Liberty Drive
Bloomington, IN 47403
www.authorhouse.com
Phone: 1-800-839-8640

Published by AuthorHouse 6/17/2013

ISBN: 978-1-4817-5899-4 (sc)
ISBN: 978-1-4817-5900-7 (hc)
ISBN: 978-1-4817-5901-4 (e)

Library of Congress Control Number: 2013909871

Dedication

To my children Tyler and Lauren and their next generation of Earthlings who will be stewards of our Planet: that they may see the Earth as a whole, know all there is to know, then do their best for all the world.

Foreword

The alien scout reported to his commander, "Sir, I have confirmed that the Earthlings possess nuclear weapons."

The alien commander asked, "Are they a threat to us?"

"No, sir," said the scout. "They have them pointed at each other."

Table of Contents

Prologue:
Song of Planet Earth
[An Alien Song]

I.

By the galactic straits of Orion Arm in Milky Way,
On a spiraling wave of space-time curvature,
Shines a yellow Sun afire with nuclear starlight.
Born out of vast nebulous dust of supernovae
Sol's gravity disk swirls silently in deepest night.
From a cloud of star matter slung into orbits tight,
Coalesced as planets waltzing on a far-flung plane,
Bright and hard are these jewels by Sun enflamed.

II.

A third planet Earth glimmering like lapis lazuli --
Its bright blue orb framed by the deep black sky
And banded in white whorls of cloud-like sinter --
Basks in a temperate zone of Sun's extremity
Where land, water and air can co-exist together.
As Earth spins in pas de deux with Moon as partner,
Its inner core brims with magmous roiling heat
To warm its surface layer to a vibrant beat.

III.

It was by chance elemental carbon of valence four,
Joining with covalent elements in water and air,
That built amino acids into functional proteins
Enabling biologic energy to be made and stored.
It was by chance the stability of nucleotides
For amine encoding of genes that replicated
Into nuclei of cells and made enzymes rife
For all the functions needed for biotic life.

IV.

Over a billion years passed in lush chemistry
Of biotic soup boiling in Earth's thermal spumes,
Permutating in organic structures of every kind
Engaged in pathways of ever growing diversity.
Biding another billion years of cellular complexity
Flourishing in rich hosts of slime, mold and fungi,
All flora and fauna emerged in genera diverse,
Producing the richness of life covering Earth.

V.

Fungal yeast captured life's basic cell best,
Encoded in DNA the same today as in man.
In paean to this cell life, humans now bless
Bread and wine fermented by ancient yeast.
Across a billion more years in waters still blue,
From Cambrian genus of worm emergent new,
Fishes filled the seas and came on land amphibian,
To rule as dinosaurs then gave way to mammalian.

VI.

For mammals sex enabled opposites to mate,
Rewarded by orgasm propelling sperm to egg,
Diversifying their gene pools with each offspring,
Selected by nature for the fittest to procreate.
Through fighting, hunting, mating, and providing,
Nature chose the strong, wily, sexy and cunning.
From tree shrew to lemur, then gibbon to bonobo,
Last emerged the upright tool-user, genus homo.

VII.

In mankind, a new order of mind emerged,
A reflection of life-affirming spirit of universe.
Man learned to transform thought into matter,
What no mind could foresee, no desire imagined.
Migrating out of Africa to far places ever greener,
Man the wise learned to seek food and find shelter,
Creating art and invention, language and writing,
To tame the wild, his knowledge ever growing.

VIII.

But man's pride led to greed, and lust to domination,
Till all the world was subject to man's deadly bidding.
In great suffering has mankind's misfortunes grown
In every age with death, disease and devastation,
From hands lifting a black flag of Mongol khan
To the same fitting krytron trigger to nuclear bomb,
Casting a dark side to what man has accomplished,
With a loss for every gain, a price paid for every wish.

IX.

What shall be the outcome of mankind on Earth?
To fall under the weight of hubris unrepentant,
Burdened by many evils on which life was spent,
Or to live in greater grace to life's true worth?
The need for warmth that desired fire to be lit,
Now burns fossil fuels clouding Earth's climate;
While the rich and powerful hoard ill-gotten wealth,
The poor and sick dwell in hunger and ill health.

X.

Already consuming Earth's resources with undue haste
Faster than can be replaced, man's seven billion
In number may double in only fifty years time,
Speeding resource depletion and mindless waste.
Can man waken from stupor and change his mind
To take needed steps and avert the end of his kind?
These are the questions to be probed on Earth today
To answer: what better nature in man will hold sway?

[EXPLORATION LOG: MILKY WAY GALAXY,
ORION ARM, LOCAL BUBBLE 8K PARSECS GC,
SOL S, 3RD PLANET, EARTH CE, 158°W,
21.5°N, 05.15.2013, 10:30:01 AM]

Call me Alvin. Some years ago – never mind how long precisely -- I decided to travel around Planet Earth to experience it as a whole. I thought I should know what it is like to be an inhabitant of Earth not limited to any one country, race, religion, ethnicity, or family. I wanted to experience the existence of all human beings as a whole, as I believe that Earth is a unique blessing bestowed on all humans, and that they have a responsibility to live on it and use its bounty accordingly. While my viewpoint may seem alien to most humans, it may in fact be important to their survival on Earth.

Planet Earth has a richness rare in this Galaxy, or almost anywhere else in the Universe for that matter. In a temperate habitable zone gently warmed by the Sun, this planet's breathable atmosphere, cool surface waters, plant-rich land masses, and magma-layered interior core all co-exist in an harmonious balance. Biologically perfected and intelligent life forms have emerged from primordial cellular life through genetic evolution driven by sexual mating of species. An upright walking hominid species with large brain capacity and dexterous appendages called "man" or "human" has developed to high self- and other-awareness.

Humans engage in diverse social interactions with each other, mostly by making differentiated verbal sounds called "speech." This enables humans to continuously communicate their state of being to others and, consequently, to monitor the status of others. Speech has positive effects, such as expressing love or caring for others, and also negative effects, such as exhibiting fear or envy of others. The history of humans reflects this duality of consciousness, positively through altruism, charity, and cooperation, and negatively through domination, war, and genocide.

In a recent global cataclysm called World War II, some sixty to seventy million humans were killed, and the conflict was ended in part by American use of its newly developed nuclear weapons against the Asian power of Japan. Following the war, the Americans and the Russians developed large arsenals of nuclear weapons as superpowers engaged in a global arms race with the potential to destroy themselves and the entire world thousands of times over. A dozen other societies sought to develop their own arsenals of nuclear weapons. In reaction to superpower dominance, rogue states and clandestine stateless combatants have also tried to acquire weapons of mass destruction to destabilize or intimidate dominant societies considered as enemies. The untoward use of nuclear weapons appears on present human course to be a risk of high probability.

Humans have a highly developed capacity of mind that, when combined with free will learned from their evolution for species survival, often causes them to act in ways contrary to the needs of their objective circumstances. Whether humans will act to avoid destruction of themselves and Earth depends on their state of mind. I decided to take a trip around Planet Earth for a study of humans to understand their ways of thinking about the dire risks they face. My trip was taken by inhabiting the mind of a world traveler as a dual consciousness surveying diverse human viewpoints around the world.

1
Japan: The First Ground Zero

[EXPLORATION LOG: EARTH CE, 140°E,
34°N, 05.16.2013, 02:30:01 PM]

Analysis of paleontological evidence and recorded histories of human beings reveals that the modern hominid species Homo Sapiens originated in Africa and began migrating out of the African continent about 100,000 years ago onto the Eurasian continent. With their adaptive physical and mental abilities for tool manipulation, discovery of how to make and control fire, and development of speech and symbol manipulation for social intercourse and status ordering, modern humans established themselves as nomadic tribes of hunter-gatherers in fertile, animal-rich regions across the Eurasian land mass, driving out and eventually exterminating other hominid species such as Neanderthal and Cro-Magnon.

With warming climate and receding glaciers ending the recent Ice Age about 20,000 years ago, human tribes grew in population and began to exhaust gatherable wood and plant resources and diminishing animal herds in their locales. They adapted by learning to raise cattle and plant and irrigate crops to produce food. In consequence, they began to organize larger human societies for controlling and managing land and water resources for food production and human habitation in established settlements.

To promote cohesion among growing populations, psychological adepts, such as shamans, advisors, and seers, took on the role of providing inspiring stories of the origin of their people, their place in the larger world, and assurance of their future survival. These "priests" became powerful stewards of the codification of societal tenets into religions, often requiring patronage, gifts and other tributes in return. A religion was useful for keeping social order, codifying status systems among people, and promoting cooperation among the various classes or castes within a society. In conflicts among competing societies, religion was also useful for branding others as infidels or evil ones, and therefore justifying their killing or subjugation. The more virulent a religion is in justifying killing or subjugating others, the more successful the society is likely to be.

Among the many religions extant among humans today, Christianity is practiced by 33% of the world population, Islam 21%, Hinduism 13%, and Buddhism 6%. The major religions all share the common vision of people aspiring to be at one with the great spirit of life in the Universe. Yet, to promote their own specialness, each religion typically advocates its own unique set of beliefs that are adopted by their followers and are used to exclude non-believers. Exclusionary beliefs make interfaith dialog and mutual understanding difficult if not impossible. Islam, now the fastest growing religion on Earth, is the most virulent in asserting that non-believers are to be converted or subjugated. Human religions, like human nature in general, tend to express high aspirations, but the actions of their believers tend to follow their own self-interests.

For my world survey of typical human states of mind, I have identified a passenger in Seat 33A on a Japan Airlines flight heading to Tokyo to join a travel group on a tour around the world. His name is Alvin, that is, Alvin Santori. Once I inhabit his mind with my dual consciousness, he should not feel uncomfortable at all since humans have some capacity for higher-order consciousness and are not unfamiliar with it, although it is not often used by them. Well, here we go!

*"Shifting into human mode to inform our survey,
Flying eight miles high over deep blue Pacific,
Embracing the mind of one named Alvin Santori,
Enroute around the world in westerly flight,
To visit great places in human deed and thought,
Together we will see what man has wrought
Over time's span and planet's green terrain,
Whether man's future is bright, or in vain."*

As the plane descended on its final approach for landing, Alvin Santori, Italian-American of Catholic background, reflexively made the Sign of the Cross over his visage. "In the name of the Father, Son and Holy Spirit, amen," he chanted in his mind as he brought together his right thumb, forefinger and middle finger and touched them to his forehead, chest, and from left to right shoulder. Doing that gave Alvin a feeling that God had blessed the airplane to land safely.

Alvin knew from his childhood education in the Catholic Church that the Sign of the Cross represented the Holy Trinity: the three personages of God manifested as the Father God of Abraham and Moses, the Son incarnate in Jesus Christ, and the Holy Spirit that instilled within the faithful. The Trinity was said at every mass to be a mystery of the Christian faith. It was in contrast to the belief in God as one person in the Judaic and Islamic religions.

Alvin read somewhere that the Sign of the Cross was a gesture adopted by early Christians to signify their faith, and commonly used to identify themselves in public. During the Crusades, Christian soldiers from different regions of the Roman Empire used it to identify themselves as Christian at a safe distance. It was rejected by Protestants during the Reformation and is not used by them. Alvin had no need to identify himself as Catholic on the airplane, but made the sign anyway. It was as if his right hand was a separate person making the sign on its own from many years of Catholic practice. The gesture was as if to say, "Ah, everything is all right with me now. How about you?"

The Japan Airlines plane landed gently on the tarmac at Narita Airport as the runway came rushing into view against a blur of hangar buildings and utility equipment. It was a gray overcast day, and the runway for taxiing was wet with rivulets casting a dull sheen of sky's pallor. A ground attendant in overalls stood in front of a terminal dock with a flashlight in each hand, left arm pointing straight left and right arm pulling vertically to signal the aircraft into the docking bay. The passengers filed out of the plane with a hush, reflexively following the polite silence maintained by the crew's Japanese attendants.

"*Shitsurei desu-ga, gaikokujin desu-ka?* (Excuse me, are you a foreigner, an alien citizen?)" chirped a smartly dressed gate attendant with a bow.

"Hai, gaikokujin desu. Yes, a foreigner," Alvin replied.

["*Hai, gaikokujin desu. Yes, an alien.*"] Alvin was startled a little and felt a slight out-of-body experience as though he were viewing himself speaking to the gate attendant from above, but quickly resettled himself in his mind.

Alvin always found it remarkable how Japanese people maintain a calm, outward civility toward strangers without betraying inner feeling, rather like a salute. Japanese speech in public is punctuated by gentle expressions of agreement and courtesy bracketed by deep bows. This is the Japanese way of warding off trouble from foreigners and strangers with politeness.

Emerging from the cavernous airport structure on the express train to Tokyo, Alvin was greeted by the sight of emerald green expanses of rice farms all along the rail line. These were the jewels of Japanese rural life. Supported by government grower subsidies and mandated domestic pricing, the rice farmers were the privileged land barons of modern Japanese society. Every rice farming village, Alvin observed, comprised elegant two and three-storied family compounds, well-maintained local schools, spacious village halls, recreational areas and communal facilities, and everywhere the green rectangular paddies sprouting rows of orderly stalks of treasured Japanese rice. This looks like it has been and will be this way forever, he thought.

About a half hour later, the placid rice fields began to give way to the sprawl of suburban communities for commuters to Tokyo. Boxy multi-family apartments populated the landscape interspersed with town market centers and malls ablaze with advertising signs, and punctuated by occasional eyesores of screen-mesh-festooned golf driving ranges and tall radio and cellphone towers.

Entering the outskirts of Tokyo, the suburban sprawl changed into vertical jumbles of postwar concrete buildings, elevated rail lines, and highway flyovers. These half-century old structures appeared soot-stained and all the same shade of gray. The bright advertising signs could barely conceal the drabness of the aging infrastructure. Toward the center of Tokyo, more modern steel-and-glass building towers came into view, then disappeared as the express train descended into the underground tunnels beneath the city proper.

After settling into a comfortable hotel room near Tokyo Station, Alvin went out in a light drizzling rain to a nearby *yakiniku-ya* for a beer and grilled snacks before going to meet the tour group at the Nihon Ginza Hotel. The cozy restaurant was filled with young adults in after-work groups chatting amiably. The gregarious *sararii-men* joked and told entertaining stories with the confidence of regulars, while the young "office ladies" exuded rapt approval and blushing admiration of these "rising stars." Later, when married, or past the age for marriage, the men would go out drinking in male-only groups with stolid faces and slumped shoulders, while the women stayed at home with children and a sharp eye on the family checkbook.

Alvin arrived a few minutes early for the tour group meeting being held in a private lounge area of the hotel. At the entrance the tour leader introduced himself as Latif Yousef. He shook hands warmly with Alvin and motioned him in to where the other tour members were gathering. An older Japanese man seated comfortably on a leather sofa introduced himself to Alvin in English as Yasuo Tanaka.

"Ah, how do you do, *Santori-san*?" chimed Mr. Tanaka. "I am joining the tour from Tokyo. Did you just arrive today? I see you have been out walking about in our usual June rains."

To match Mr. Tanaka's use of the *san* honorific with his last name, Alvin also used the honorific to address Mr. Tanaka. "*Hai, Tanaka-san*, it certainly is nice to be back on the ground. The flight over was very smooth. I must confess that I've been out for a little beer and *tsukune*, which does wonders for jetlag!" Alvin replied.

Alvin told Mr. Tanaka that he was a lawyer working with a foreign affairs think-tank based in Hawaii, mainly on studies for the Arms Control Institute in Washington D.C.

"Oh, what kind of foreign affairs do you study?" asked Mr. Tanaka.

"It's a bit specialized, having to do with policies to prevent the spread of nuclear weapons."

"*Ah, so desu ne, muzukashii desu ne.* (Oh, yes, very difficult work.)" Mr. Tanaka found Alvin's work to be of great interest, as he had grown up in Tokyo during the postwar years. He remembered the terrible stories of many people suffering in the aftermath of the bombings of cities by the U.S. that forced Japan to surrender to end World War II. But he quickly changed the subject, rather than dwell on those memories.

"As for myself, I retired as an engineer from Sumitomo Electric Company about ten years ago, and now have a taste for traveling. I visited Hawaii a while ago when my daughter and son-in-law decided to hold their wedding there. I remember the beaches were so clean and the ocean waters so clear and warm."

"Yes," Alvin rejoined, "and I have visited Japan to enjoy the refreshing waters of your mountain *onsen*. And your *sake* brewed with the freshest of spring waters. It seems that so many truly enjoyable things in life have to do with water."

A tall blond woman with a self-possessed, educated look introduced herself as Jane Ferrara and her traveling companion Ralph McAlister. "We were scheduled to attend a conference in Edinburgh on alternative methods for teaching music. When we heard that this around-the-world tour included a stop in Edinburgh on the same date, we decided to go on the tour. It makes it all the more wonderful!"

Jane was a striking woman of mature years, with a lilting style of inflection that made her sound a bit like a dilettante. But one could sense otherwise by her alert manner of speaking and careful listening to others. Her lilting voice and discernment of the voices of others probably grew out of her lifelong work teaching music. In complete contrast Ralph appeared to be a laid-back naturally-stoned jazz musician. He did not overtly show his musical tendencies, such as by tapping out rhythms or humming riffs. Instead, he liked to keep his hands busy with careful and precise work, such as the way he arranged his papers and belongings in his knapsack and touched each of the contents in his saxophone case before stowing it.

A man in his early forties appearing to be of Middle-Eastern descent stood by himself at the periphery of those introducing themselves. He did not seem unfriendly, just a bit nervous or shy. Izfahan Ghazen said that he was an Egyptian national who became a U.S. citizen while doing computer research at a U.S. company. He had a piercing gaze that in Middle-Easterners is taken either as reflecting a high intelligence or religious fanaticism, or both.

"Hi," said Alvin going up to him, "I'm Alvin Santori, a lawyer and foreign affairs writer from Hawaii. What brings you on this trip?"

"Oh, hi, I'm Izfahan Ghazen," he said warming up on being addressed. "You can call me Iz. I work with a defense contractor MicroSimulation Systems in San Francisco." Iz paused a moment looking professional, then relaxed. "We just finished a big project and the company wanted us to take some of our vacation time for R and R. My daughter is in summer camp for a couple of months, and my wife wanted to go to a family wedding in Cairo. I don't like hot weather and I'm not good hanging out with tons of relatives, so here I am."

"Sounds like this trip will be a perfect respite from business and family at just the right time," said Alvin. "I love it when things work out that way. For me, my wife wanted to take my daughter to spend time with relatives in California and do a swim camp, so I jumped at the opportunity to take this trip."

Latif called the meeting to order and went over details of the tour for the next six weeks. He mentioned, though trying to be modest, that he was an internationally recognized Sufi musician and poet, originally from Turkey, who now resided in San Francisco. He grew up in Turkey, majoring in mathematics at the prestigious Middle Eastern Technical University in Ankara, and studied music at the Julliard School in New York City. For the past several years he has led private tours to his native Turkey and other key historical and cultural places around the world. Most of his guests heard about his tours when he gave concerts and readings around the U.S. every year.

The other travelers introduced themselves. John and Barbara Hadley were retired teachers from Santa Fe. Don Overton was a senior executive at a wine distribution company, and he and his wife Meredith lived in Portland, Oregon. Lee Cheng was a Chinese-born naturalized citizen working in the import-export business in San Francisco.

Dressed in an impeccable Chanel suit, a demure and composed woman introduced herself as Akiko Sato. She briefly recounted that she was originally from Japan, went to American Catholic School in Tokyo, studied biochemistry at Stanford, then married an American research scientist and had two children. She was now widowed and living alone in San Francisco since her children graduated from college. Alvin overheard Latif say that her husband had been a defense researcher in high-energy physics who passed away unexpectedly from cancer.

Latif gave the tour group a quick summary of the tour's itinerary to Tokyo, Hiroshima, Beijing, Mongolia, a land-tour of Turkey, Istanbul, Edinburgh, Barcelona, New York, and ending in San Francisco. After handling the tour details and the excited questions of the travelers, Latif guided everyone out for the group's first dinner together at a nearby *shabu-shabu* restaurant.

The next morning, the tour group visited the Yasukuni Shrine in the center of Tokyo, a memorial to Japan's war dead in World War II. The Shrine was considered controversial because Japanese militarists who were convicted and executed as war criminals were among the honored war dead. Japanese officials and politicians have been heavily criticized in the world press for ceremonial visits to the Shrine. Latif confided to the group that he had chosen the Yasukuni Shrine to start the tour because it showed how a country that went to war with the U.S. can have a completely opposite point of view of the same circumstances.

The quiet halls of the Shrine were lined with exhibits and photographs extolling the heroic and patriotic deeds of Japan's military in the war. It clearly represented a one-sided view, but was understandable when one saw each person proud of service to their country in the photographs and mementos. Every man was someone's husband, father, or son, and every one of them clearly loved his country Japan.

In a small high-ceilinged room that was at the center of the surrounding galleries, a simple and elegant display evoked reverence for those who died in the war. At the four corners of the room were four wall hangings of gauzy fabric, and on each was written in calligraphy a poetic saying taken from among the letters or writings of the dead. The poems were simple statements of self-sacrifice, love of country, love of Emperor, and acceptance of death. Those who were Japanese in the room took deep bows before each display. Many stood for long moments in silent reverence, some sobbing audibly.

Alvin sidled over and quietly asked Mr. Tanaka, "Does this Shrine mean that the Japanese feel they were justified in going to war?"

"No," Mr. Tanaka replied slowly, "this Shrine does not glorify Japan's involvement in the war. It is intended to honor those who sacrificed their lives for their Emperor and country. Two million Japanese soldiers died at war, and half a million civilians died in the Allied bombing of our cities. Imperial Japan was blinded by its successes in modernizing and militarily in Asia after the Meiji emperor's restoration. They inflicted tens of millions of casualties on others, and some of the worst atrocities are finally being officially acknowledged. While a nationalistic fringe might never accept making a national apology, most Japanese do feel a sense of remorse and a deep lesson never again to resort to war. I grew up during the aftermath of the war and know firsthand how the survivors suffered. It was as if we needed to endure those hardships to atone for our sins. But the Japanese people cannot disavow their past with dishonor, so this Shrine is a necessity, even though it may be detested by others."

Outside the museum the group visited a Shinto temple on the grounds of the Yasukuni Shrine. Mr. Tanaka demonstrated to the others how to approach the temple altar and make a motion with the hands in prayer and clap to awaken the spirit world to receive one's supplications. He blushed at sharing a Japanese spiritual ritual with foreigners. To many Japanese like Mr. Tanaka, Shinto rituals only seemed proper when practiced by Japanese.

Alvin wondered at Mr. Tanaka's openness in sharing a Shinto ritual with foreigners on the tour group. It seemed that all religions made friendly gestures of sharing the promise of spiritual salvation with others, yet all espoused doctrines that differentiated between "we chosen ones" and outsiders. In the Catholic Church, sharing was expressed by the greeting "all are welcome" yet only confirmed Catholics were welcome to receive the bread symbolizing "the body of Christ" in the holiest part of a Eucharist mass. Alvin could remember incidents when persons who stood up for communion but did not perform the ritual holding of hands in supplication, crossing themselves or genuflecting were accosted by church attendants with an icy query "Are you Catholic?"

Later the tour group visited the Asakusa district of Tokyo, one of the oldest villages that formed the Edo capital of feudal Japan. As the guests emerged from the subway exit, they heard the huge roaring of thousands of people lining the major street that passed in front of the Asakusa Kannon Temple Senso-ji. Mr. Tanaka shouted to the others that this was the high festival day of the Sanja Matsuri, one of the three great Shinto festivals in Tokyo. Swept up with a mass of singing and dancing people, they could see the top of a large wooden *mikoshi* shrine ahead, swaying as its great weight was carried down the street on poles supported on the shoulders of a hundred chanting men dressed in festival *yukata*, their bare legs and slippered feet moving in wave motion like a millipede. The bearers shook and bounced the portable shrine vigorously, as if to make the *kami* spirits seated in a shrouded palanquin at the top of the shrine nod and gesticulate to the masses of delirious people lining each block to bestow good luck on all. In all there must have been over a million people flooding the streets and vendor alleys all around Asakusa, and the din of flutes, whistles, chanting and *taiko* drums sat like a dense cloud over the whole area.

Mr. Tanaka shouted to the tour group that three grand *mikoshi* are paraded on the final day of the festival. Each is built to look like a miniature version of the Asakusa Temple, decorated with gold sculptures and painted with gold leaf, and each weighing about one ton. In an investiture ritual, three *kami* spirits revered as patron spirits of the Asakusa Temple are invited into the miniature shrines where they reside for the duration of the festival. The three *mikoshi* are taken along different routes to bestow blessings on all the districts of Asakusa. In the evening, the three shrines are returned to the Asakusa Temple in grand processions that last late into the night.

"Why do the people become so delirious just from these symbols of patron spirits passing in the street?" Iz asked Mr. Tanaka.

"They are believed to bestow good luck on all the people they come into contact with. To a Japanese person, a visible sign of their deities bestowing symbolic good luck feels like one is actually receiving good luck. This turns all of one's fears and misfortunes into good blessings for the future, and this makes one's deepest feeling happy," said Mr. Tanaka.

"There certainly is nothing like this in the Catholic religion," said Alvin. "The closest thing I can think of in Christianity is the singing worship of parishioners in the Pentacostal Church which can produce ecstatic experiences, healing miracles, or speaking in tongues."

"There is definitely nothing like this in Islam. We worship Allah as one God and God of all. There are no other deities, and no deity symbol can represent Allah. Ecstatic experiences may happen in Islam when revering the one God of all, or perhaps in singing the scriptures of the Koran," said Latif.

"Yes," agreed Iz. "Islam seeks to avoid religious-induced experiences that divert or mask one's true experience of God. It seeks to be a pure religion, in that sense. Yet, I do find it intriguing that a religion like Shinto can bring on religious ecstasy in believers such as in the Matsuri."

The next day, the tour group took a *Shinkansen* bullet train to Kyoto then a local train to Nara, Japan's ancient capital from the third century CE and official seat of the Shinto religion. In the late afternoon, they visited the Todai-ji Temple, the largest wooden building in the world, which houses the Daibutsu, or Great Buddha, one of the largest bronze statues in the world. A stroll through Nara Park from Todai-ji took them to the Kasuga Grand Shrine of Shinto and nearby Kofukuji Temple representing the Shinto-Buddhist fusion before the Meiji restoration.

Alvin walked with Mr. Tanaka and Akiko around the historic site. "It seems that all these shrines represent a perfect harmony in feeling of the Japanese people for God," he said, and added, "despite Shinto and Buddhism being different religions."

"Japanese people are brought up to revere their ancestors and to seek harmony with the spiritual realm," explained Mr. Tanaka. "Religious practice provides an entry to the spiritual realm, but there can be many entrances. It is not unusual for a Japanese to adopt several religious practices together if they provide comfortable ways to access one's spiritual nature."

"How do you feel about it, having grown up in Japan and being educated and living in the U.S.?" Alvin asked Akiko.

She pursed her lips and gave his question some thought. "Being conversant with the unseen as well as what is visible makes one a more balanced person, I think. For myself I prefer personal ways to address the spiritual world other than religion, such as reading wonderful poetry, or listening to an inspired piece of music, or even just having a conversation with a friend who listens with their whole mind."

Alvin smiled at hearing this. Even though she said little and seemingly preferred to keep to herself while with the tour group, he was beginning to like her very much.

The following day the tour group woke early to take the train to Hiroshima where they would stay for two days. They first visited the Hiroshima Peace Memorial Park dedicated to the memory of victims of the first city in the world to suffer an atomic bomb attack on August 6, 1945. The Peace Park was built on a large open field that was Ground Zero for the explosion of the aerial bomb codenamed "Little Boy" having an energy equivalent of fifteen thousand tons of TNT. A large, grass-covered knoll called the Memorial Mound reportedly contained the ashes of some seventy thousand people killed directly by the bomb. At the epicenter of the blast site stood the "A-Bomb Dome," the skeletal metal ribbing of what was once the dome of the Industrial Promotion Hall. A sign said that this was "a sacred site in remembrance of ultimate catastrophe, and a symbol of hope for world peace."

Near the center of the park was a concrete cenotaph bearing the names of persons killed by the atomic bomb. The epitaph said simply, "Rest in Peace, for the error shall not be repeated." Nearby was the Peace Flame that remains lit continuously "until all nuclear bombs on the planet are destroyed and the planet is free from the threat of nuclear annihilation." The Peace Bell hung in an adjacent, open-sided structure. Visitors were encouraged to ring the bell for world peace, and the loud and melodious tolling of the bell rang out regularly throughout the park. The bell bore inscriptions in Greek, Japanese, and Sanskrit for "Know Thyself," quoted from the Greek philosopher Socrates.

While the group sipped tea at a park refreshment area, Latif recounted some of the history of Japan leading to the occasion for the Peace Park. With the Meiji Restoration in 1867 ending the Tokugawa Shogunate and restoring the Emperor Meiji to absolute power, Japan embarked on a vast program to arm itself and adopt advanced Western technologies. Its military undertook an expansionist drive to establish colonies in Asia to supply Japan with oil, metal ores, timber, human labor and other resources. When Nazi Germany began the war in 1939 to subjugate Europe and Eurasia, Japan seized the opportunity to establish hold over the Asia-Pacific region by attacking the U.S. Pacific Fleet based at Pearl Harbor in Hawaii. World War II was characterized by acts of extraordinary brutality and widespread human carnage estimated to total seventy million deaths worldwide. The Japanese army in particular inflicted massive casualties and widespread atrocities on civilian populations. Its soldiers were indoctrinated to kill themselves rather than surrender.

Spurred by earlier rumors that Germany was working to develop a nuclear weapon, and facing massive casualties trying to defeat an army that would not surrender, the United States undertook a crash program codenamed the "Manhattan Project" in 1942 to develop the world's first atomic bomb. It was a crude design using a gun-type explosive actuator and fissile uranium target. The fifteen-kiloton bomb dropped on Hiroshima is estimated to have caused total deaths of one-hundred-forty thousand people killed by the blast and later from radiation sickness and disease. A second, implosion-type bomb nicknamed "Fat Man" was dropped on Nagasaki three days later. It had an explosive yield of twenty-one kilotons but, due to Nagasaki's hilly terrain, the damage was less extensive than in relatively flat Hiroshima. An estimated thirty-nine thousand people were killed outright and a further twenty-five thousand later died of radiation sickness. Less than a week after, Emperor Hirohito announced the surrender of Japan.

Alvin reflected on the act of massive incineration of unprecedented numbers of people that led to the solemn wish for world peace by the surviving victims memorialized in the Peace Park. The U.S. decision to use the atomic bomb on a civilian population was justified by government authorities as necessary to save the lives of tens of thousands of U.S. soldiers that would need to be expended that year to finally defeat the Japanese military to end the war in the Pacific. Yet many consider the use of the first weapons of mass destruction against civilian populations a war crime that violated the International Geneva Convention at the highest level. The practicality of the U.S. decision was compelled only by the U.S. strategic plan to drive the Japanese military from islands in the East China Sea north to the Japanese main islands.

"I guess justification for a horrific act can always be made to seem compelling if a worse alternative can be conjured up by comparison," said Alvin. "Perhaps this is what the surviving victims here learned. Their prayer for world peace goes to the heart of the matter, to avoid violence from escalating into the death spiral of justification."

"But hoping for peace does not seem to bring about peace," observed Iz. "Quite the contrary, it can convey weakness, and being weak invites violence. Notice that since Hiroshima there are many more countries that now possess or want to acquire nuclear weapons."

"That is a major dilemma of our era," said Alvin. "The fact is that nuclear weapons are surprisingly easy to build once enriched uranium or fissile plutonium is available. Both of these materials can be obtained from irradiated nuclear fuel used in nuclear reactors, which have a supposed 'peaceful' use for generating electricity. More and more nations will need to turn to nuclear reactors for electricity as the world's oil supplies peak and coal burning needs to be curtailed due to global warming. So more reactors everywhere means more opportunities to acquire nuclear material."

From his arms control work, Alvin offered the group a brief summary of how nuclear weapons have proliferated since its first use by the U.S. on Japan. The U.S. success provoked the Soviet Union to accelerate its own development of nuclear weapons. Starting with a first test in 1949, Russian development escalated to explosion of the largest thermonuclear bomb ever at fifty megatons in 1961. In the so-called Cold War, Russia and the U.S. vied to build up their arsenals of nuclear weapons, reaching well over 20,000 warheads on each side by the 1980s. Russia also transferred the knowledge to make nuclear weapons to China, its Communist ally against the United States.

The U.S. and Russia each sought to deter a first strike by the other by threatening massive retaliation through a surviving second-strike capability of many times more missiles dispersed in submarines, trains, trucks, tunnels and underground silos. With each side having a second-strike capability, it became clear that any nuclear strike by one would result in mutual annihilation or "mutually assured destruction" of both. The resulting global radioactive miasma and induced climate change would be catastrophic for the planet as a whole.

The United Kingdom became the third nuclear-armed nation in 1952 building an arsenal of reportedly two hundred warheads. France tested its first nuclear weapon in 1960 and maintains a stockpile of some three hundred warheads. With assistance from Russia, China became the fifth nuclear nation in 1964 and maintains an arsenal of reportedly two hundred warheads.

The five nuclear-armed nations drafted and became the first signatories of the Nuclear Non-Proliferation Treaty in 1968 calling for cooperative efforts to prevent the spread of nuclear weapons, reduce warhead stockpiles through gradual disarmament, and support the peaceful uses of nuclear power. The International Atomic Energy Agency (IAEA), an independent agency under auspices of the United Nations, is charged with monitoring nuclear development programs in countries of the world.

Israel was suspected to have built its first nuclear weapons in 1969, but adopted a policy of never officially admitting to having them. It is estimated to have an arsenal of some two hundred warheads deliverable by ground, aircraft, and submarine.

India tested its first nuclear device in 1974 and maintains an estimated ninety warheads. Its arch-enemy Pakistan conducted its first nuclear tests in 1983 and maintains a growing arsenal numbering well over a hundred nuclear warheads.

With assistance from Pakistan, North Korea conducted its first nuclear test in 2006, and reportedly has processed enough fissile material for six to eight bombs. The latest test is believed to have been a precursor to a compact design for use on long-range missiles that can reach the U.S., its declared enemy.

South Africa, Myanmar, Syria, Iraq, Libya, and Iran all started programs to develop nuclear weapons. South Africa abandoned its program following the changeover from its former apartheid government and signed the Nuclear Non-Proliferation Treaty in 1991. After thirty years of clandestine attempts, Libya eventually relinquished its nuclear weapons program. Nuclear weapons enabling facilities under development in Syria and later in Iraq were bombed by Israel and disabled. After starting to build a reactor for plutonium extraction with North Korea's help, Myanmar notified the IAEA in 2002 that it would instead build one for civilian use with Russian assistance. Iran is believed to have restarted enriching uranium for a nuclear weapon in 2007, and has since steadfastly maintained its right to pursue nuclear weapons development free of international monitoring.

Nuclear weapons have also been shared with non-nuclear countries by nuclear-armed countries. The U.S has based many nuclear weapons in NATO countries such as Belgium, Germany, Italy, Netherlands, Turkey, and Greece. Canada also maintained shared nuclear weapons from the U.S. until 1984. The Soviet Union based nuclear weapons in Belarus, Kazakhstan, and Ukraine until its collapse in 1991 compelled it to withdraw them.

Alvin paused to see how his account of nuclear arms history was being received by the tour group.

"Hey Alvin," said Iz, "you want to hear a joke about nuclear weapons?"

"Sure," Alvin grinned, "it would be a relief from this somber history."

"These aliens were scoping out Planet Earth and checking out the human race. One alien scout reported to their commander, 'Humans on Earth have developed nuclear weapons in many countries.' 'Really, are they a threat to us?' asked the alien commander. 'Nah, they got them pointed at each other,' came the scout's reply."

"Ha-ha-ha," Alvin laughed, "that's a good one, Iz."

[*"It seems more true than funny."*]

The others in the tour group did not laugh with Alvin. They seemed still in shock at hearing how prevalent nuclear weapons had become around the world, and horrified at the consequences of the single atomic bombing, a small one no less, that they saw memorialized at the Peace Park.

That night, the tour group enjoyed a dinner over *sake* rice wine and grilled *okonomiyaki*, Hiroshima style. But behind the smiles and convivial talk, their eyes looked sad as they reflected on the horrors of nuclear war that they learned about during the day. The dinner broke up early so everyone could get a good night's rest for the next segment of the trip to Beijing in the morning.

2
China: A Global Disaster in the Making

[EXPLORATION LOG: EARTH CE, 113°E, 19°N, 05.22.2013, 04:00:01 PM]

As humans increase in population from seven billion now to over ten billion projected by Year 2050, while depleting available resources to meet expanding living needs, will they be able to sustain themselves without devolving into global territorial and resource conflicts? Humans as a whole need far less than they consume currently. Over seventy-five percent of material sold as consumer products is thrown away as garbage or dumped into landfills. Food is widely wasted or mal-distributed, and potable water is overused and used water is needlessly discharged as polluted. Humans could meet all of their needs even with a population of more than ten billion if their materials, food and water could be better used, distributed, recycled, and recovered.

Energy, food and water resources for human needs could be made abundantly available globally. The Sun delivers photonic energy daily to land and thermal warming to ocean waters equal to ten thousand times the energy that humans use, and this energy could be tapped with known technologies if humans would price their usage of fossil fuels at their true depletion, pollution, and global warming costs. Abundant food resources could be produced by more efficient farming on land and aquaculture in the oceans. Abundant water resources could be produced by water recovery on land and desalination of ocean waters if human political systems could provide for infrastructure and equitable distribution.

Yet humans in general seem inclined to take perverse actions opposite from common sense when it comes to meeting human needs. In democratic societies, well-off people want greater accumulation of wealth and status symbols, drawing resources away from equitable use for the poor. Middle-income people are marketed needless or repetitively substitute goods to keep the economy growing and become trapped when their real incomes cannot keep pace with inflating costs. Governments try to mitigate growing economic pain and political discontent in the short term by borrowing into debt or inflating their currency, leading to a worsening economic crisis later. Politicians try to ensure their own survival by playing the blame game on opposing parties, so that necessary political action becomes deadlocked. Non-democratic societies follow a similar spiral into perversity by command.

When it becomes impossible to unwind the spiral of perverse behavior politically, humans have sought to overthrow their governments with new ideologies to provide for their needs. Human imagination has invented new technologies to better extract needed resources from the Earth, but generally this is done in a race without care for pollution and waste, the costs for which are consequently pushed onto the lesser developed of the world's populations. Fringe groups may seek to break the logjam of status quo by espousing extreme views that incite violence. Countering violence would require increased military and policing costs that drain resources away from meeting basic human needs. Violence can escalate to wars causing widespread devastation, famine, and disease. The survey needs to investigate whether the perversely managed growth of human needs risks a death spiral for humans into global war and destruction.

The tour group took a morning flight from Tokyo to Guangzhou, the first of three cities in China next on the tour. Their plane flew over the Japan Alps, across the Japan Sea, and along the eastern coast of the

Chinese mainland to the South China Sea. Under a clear morning sky, Alvin could see the reflected sunlight glittering on the coastal waters of the Pacific Ocean lapping up against the continental landmass of Asia. It all seemed so beautiful and peaceful flying six miles high above the coastline.

Latif gave the tour group a quick sketch of the history of China, and the Han people at its core, the oldest continuous civilization on Earth. The Han genetic haplotype is traceable to origins thirty-five thousand years ago in eastern China along the Yellow River. Referred to in genealogical circles as "The Inventors," the Han people are credited with originating many practical inventions still in use today, such as paper, gunpowder, the toothbrush, and the compass.

"The word 'Han' refers to the people being as numerous as the stars in our galaxy. The Chinese name for the Milky Way galaxy means 'Heavenly River,'" Latif informed the group.

["We are all people of the Heavenly River!"]

"We are all people as numerous as the stars!" Alvin smiled at the thought, but was a bit surprised with it coming to his mind. Astronomy was not one of his personal interests. The phrase was more familiar from the biblical account of God's promise to Abraham, the progenitor of His chosen people.

Latif continued to recount that the period of the Han dynasty from the second century BCE through second century CE was considered a golden age in Chinese history. The Han military campaigns expanded their domain into Western China and Central Asia, and established the vast overland trade network known as the Silk Road, which reached to the Mediterranean world. The Han dynasty eventually fragmented after a declining period of civil turmoil, and was replaced by the Tang dynasty in the seventh century. Following a devastating civil war, the Tang dynasty went into decline and was succeeded by the Song dynasty lasting from the tenth century into the thirteenth century. The Song lost control of northern China to the Jin dynasty and retreated from their capital on the Yellow River to the lands south of the Yangtze River. The Southern Song ruled the southerly sixty percent of China's population until their defeat by Genghis Khan's son Kublai Khan five centuries later.

"I think the civil war you referred to during the Tang dynasty was known as the An Lushan Rebellion in which an estimated thirty-six million people died," said Lee.

"Yes, historians have shown that it was a civil war with killing on a previously unimaginable scale. As one measure, a Tang census taken in 754 CE recorded a population of fifty-three million, whereas a census taken in 764 recorded seventeen million," Latif noted. "That is a huge loss of life in one decade, two of every three persons in China, probably the most devastating civil war in human history. Curiously, the Tang general An Lushan who led the rebellion was an adoptee of a Persian father and a Turkic mother from a remote western province. A Turkic rebellion among the Uighurs aligned the western provinces with An Lushan's armies controlling the lands north of the Yellow River. When An Lushan seized the Tang capital at Chang'an, a reported one million loyalists were killed, one of every two persons in the city. But the besieged Tang generals enlisted the support of Turkic mercenaries of the Uighurs sent by the Abbasid caliph al-Mansur, and their combined forces drove An Lushan out from Chang'an and back north of the Yellow River."

"So the mass killings of the Mongols later were actually not the first time China had seen slaughter on the scale of entire populations," observed Lee.

"Yes, it seems that during those feudal periods, the only way to completely remove the threat of rebellion was to kill all of those who might rebel," replied Latif.

Latif continued his history of China with Kublai Khan starting the Yuan dynasty after the defeat of the Jin and the Southern Song to rule all of China as a khanate of the Mongol empire. The Han people became infused with Mongol culture and, through Silk Road trade and intercourse, with the diverse cultures making up the Mongol empire spanning the Eurasian continent. However, after only a hundred years of rule, the Yuan dynasty devolved into regicide and was pushed out by the Ming in the fourteenth century. The Ming dynasty was known for a long reign of stability and economic prosperity, and for expansion of trade with the West.

"It is interesting that as much as the Silk Road brought goods from Chinese culture to the West, it also infused China with ideas from the West," said Iz.

"Yes, and it happened in a totally unforeseen way. Kublai Khan had met Nicolo Polo, Marco Polo's father, and Matteo Polo, his uncle, on one of their Silk Road trips. When they brought young Marco Polo along on their next trip, the Great Khan invited him to stay at his palace as a cultural advisor. Marco Polo stayed in China for seventeen years, many of which were spent on trips around China providing the Great Khan with assessments of his Chinese subjects as seen from a Western perspective. Through the Polos, Kublai Khan developed a keen interest in the Latin world, especially in Christianity. He reportedly sent a letter written in Latin back with the Polos inviting the Pope to send missionaries to convert the followers of primitive religions in China, who the Polos called 'idolators', to Christianity."

"It's a good thing Nicolo and Matteo Polo were never able to get an audience with the Pope to deliver the Khan's invitation, " laughed Latif. "Otherwise, we would have to add genocide instigated by Holy Roman Christian missionaries to China's history."

The tour group arrived at Guangzhou international airport in the late afternoon and was totally unprepared for the scenes of pedestrian crowds and traffic chaos they encountered in the rush-hour trip from the airport to their hotel. It was a sweltering day in the middle of monsoon season, and the humid subtropical climate was stifling. Weaving in and out of makeshift lines of cars jammed tightly together, the airport limo bus at last pulled up to the famed White Swan Hotel in the Liwan coastal district where the group would be staying.

Latif gave the tour group a brief history of Guangzhou, which has long been a major seaport in the south of China. Guangzhou's earliest known name was Panyu, and its recorded history began with

Han conquest of the area during the Qin Dynasty. Panyu's influence expanded and it became the capital of the Nanyue Kingdom which included the southern coastal areas down to what is now Vietnam. The Han annexed the Nanyue Kingdom in 111 BCE, and Panyu became the provincial capital. As the seat of Guang Prefecture, Panyu gradually came to be known as Guangzhou by its prefectural name.

Arab and Persian merchants were known to conduct trade in Guangzhou since the eighth century by direct sea routes from the Middle East. Portuguese explorers were the first Europeans to arrive in Guangzhou by sea in the early sixteenth century. They were granted a trade concession that they called "Canton," but were later expelled from there and granted use of Macau instead. The Portuguese concession on foreign trade in the region continued as a monopoly until the arrival of the Dutch in the early seventeenth century. When the Qing government expanded the opening of China to more foreign trade in the eighteenth century, Guangzhou became the principal seaport in China for international trade. Today Guangzhou is the capital and largest city of the Guangdong province, with a population of over fifteen million. It is the principal part of the Pearl River Delta area, which has a total population of about forty million in a land area smaller than New Jersey.

The Liwan district was the original seaport district of Canton. Over the next two days, Latif took the tour group to many important attractions and historical sites of the famed seaport. They visited the Xiguan Folk Custom Area, Chen Clan Temple Cultural Area, Shamian Continental Tourist Area, and Shisanhang Commercial and Cultural Area. Over the whole port area there were hundreds of wholesale markets, some occupying whole city blocks, selling clothing, jewelry, ceramics, traditional Chinese medicines, aquatic products, shoes, stationery, metal wares, textiles, electrical appliances, decorative materials, and so on. Throughout it all, thousands of people were pushing and shoving their way around every road, alley, and awning to haggle for goods of every description. Many streets were arrayed with shops all devoted to one type of product, such as blackwood streets, jade streets, and ceramic crafts streets.

Finally, unable to take any more, Latif signalled the group toward a tea parlor to have some *dim sum* dumplings for lunch and to rest their weary feet. As the group neared the tea parlor, they could hear a loud roar coming from within. It sounded like a riot of shouting. As they opened the doors, they were hit by a blast of sound louder than the loudest rock concert. By sign language, Latif shrugged and gestured that this was normal for noontime tea in Guangzhou. No one could hear a word anyone else said over the whole lunch.

"It's no wonder everyone was shouting," Alvin laughed, after the tour group struggled their way back to the hotel. "That is what happens when everyone wants to be heard, and no one is restrained by etiquette."

"This is why China is my least desirable place to visit," groused Jane. "There are just too many people, haggling everywhere for the most ordinary of things, and doing so without a shred of politeness or regard for personal space."

"Yes, that may be true, but you have to give the Chinese credit for making their society workable at all, said Lee Cheng, the Chinese-American businessman in the tour group. "It is the oldest civilization on Earth, lasting over twenty-five dynasties or complete eras of governance, compared to the single dynasty of U.S. democratic constitutional history of only two hundred and fifty years. Today it has a population five times that of the U.S., but with much less arable land area for food, water resources, and mineral resources. In the last thirty years of economic reform, China has lifted five hundred million people, one-third of its massive population, out of poverty to a modern standard of living."

"Well, why couldn't they act to control their population growth in the first place?" Jane countered.

"Having children is probably the most precious of life's gifts for human beings," replied Lee. "Throughout history, there have been only two effective ways to control the human birth rate. Either you have wars that kill off the unwanted populations, or you have economic and social advancement within which couples, and women especially, choose to have less children. China is the only society on Earth to implement non-violent social policies to force families to have only one child, and it suffered a strong social backlash as a result. It is now paying a steep price in unintended consequences after one generation, such as only-child spoiledness, too many males and too few females for marriage, and the population base shifting toward senior citizens retired from productive work."

Jane had to admit the truth of what Lee said, but she was not giving up. "Well, you would think that with so many people in so little space, the Chinese over their long history would have developed some minimum of social graces for conducting themselves in public. Look at the bruises on my arms from being elbowed while walking on the street, not to mention being shoved in the back into oncoming traffic while waiting at a traffic light," Jane complained.

"I know from experience that the shove in the back was actually exquisitely well-timed to get you moving in front a split second before the light turned to go. As for sharp elbows, one learns to hold your arms akimbo like this, to ward off being elbowed somewhere soft," Lee laughed. "The Chinese have learned that a bit of aggressiveness is necessary to carry on one's daily activities. But the Chinese way is to do what is necessary while striving for stability and harmony at heart."

"Ah, so. Confucius say, harmony at heart comes from long history," Alvin laughed. While having had the same emotional reactions as Jane to Chinese public behavior, Alvin appreciated seeing the view from the "other side" that Lee offered.

Latif remarked that despite being so densely populated and still having a standard of living well below advanced countries, the Chinese people have generally rated themselves as happy and satisfied with their lives. Cultivated by Taoist and Buddhist traditions and infused with Confucian moral principles, the Chinese seem to feel satisfied with the world as it is, while at the same time motivated to improve their society as a whole. However, the younger generations are starting to turn away from the traditional ethic and demanding a better lifestyle and their share of economic success.

With a population of 1.7 billion people and a long history of dynastic rule, China is compelled to maintain absolute political control while trying as best as it can to achieve continued economic growth and improvement in standard of living for all through pragmatic policies. Economic progress has become a national purpose and is unstoppable. China is well past Japan as the world's second largest economy, and expects to overtake the United States as the world's largest economy well before 2020.

With high economic growth comes high demand for electrical power and building materials like cement, both of which are the worst contributors to global warming gases that become trapped in the atmosphere. Eighty percent of China's power generation comes from coal-fired power plants, and electricity usage is expected to double by 2020. China's rate of cement production is already one-half of all cement production in the world, and is still growing. With continued growth, China is expected to account for over thirty percent of the world's total carbon emissions by 2020, almost doubling its current output at a time when climate monitoring agencies have called for a seventeen percent reduction by 2020 to pull back from irreversible climate change.

Other developing countries also want to achieve the same success in lifting people out of poverty that China has. Of the three billion increase in world population expected by 2050, over half is projected to come from India, Pakistan, Bangladesh, and major African countries. India's population is expected to exceed China's by 2050, and it wants to lift one billion people out of poverty to middle class living standards in that time. While targeting to match the improvement in living standards of China, the developing world's populations aspire to the same lavish lifestyle that Western countries now have. This would simply be impossible to sustain on the finite living resources available on Earth.

The resulting carbon emissions from such economic growth would certainly push the planet past the tipping point to irreversible climate change. Scientists have projected that an atmospheric temperature increase of just four degrees Fahrenheit in this century would result in an unstoppable cycle of polar ice melting, flooding of coastal areas, rising atmospheric temperatures, shrinking forested and vegetated areas needed for carbon sequestration, and increasingly severe weather extremes of droughts and storms. They say this could eventually result in the Earth having boiling air temperatures in the hundreds of degrees and thick choking clouds smothering all human life, a scenario they refer to pejoratively as "the Venus syndrome."

"Carbon-based economic growth is like a catastrophic bomb that explodes with a slow but unstoppable blast that increases over generations," Alvin said, following Latif's comments.

"Yet the developing world cannot stop the climate change bomb from going off because they are only trying to attain a basic standard of living," replied Latif.

"The Chinese people aspire only to provide for basic living needs, not lavish things," said Lee. "It's just that when you multiply a small desire over 1.7 billion people, it adds up to huge numbers. Everything in China must be done on a massive scale, so the attendant problems are massive. Anytime you try to improve things for 1.7 billion people, you are always just one step away from politically explosive shortages."

"Even in the U.S. my daughter's Chinese school is typical," continued Lee. "It has two hundred students, five teachers, and the only recreation at school is one ping pong table. Everything in China is like that."

"Well, at least you're not saying there is only one ping pong paddle!" laughed Iz.

"True, but the one ball they have is dented," Lee answered in all seriousness.

After several days of squeezing through Guangzhou's crowds in humid tropical weather, the tour group was glad to leave and fly to Xi'an, a beautiful walled town in the north central part of China. At an average elevation of thirteen hundred feet on the forested slopes of the Feng River valley, the climate in Xi'an was dry and cool. The serene atmosphere within the historic town reflected an authenticity and sense of permanence of its three thousand year history.

At dinner that evening, Latif informed the group that the area to the northwest of Xi'an was chosen by the first emperor of China, Qin Shi Huang, to be the first imperial capital of China. Emperor Qin ended the Zhou dynasty and conquered the major states extant from the Warring States Period to unify China as an empire in 221 BCE. By abolishing the power of landowning lords, directly enlisting peasants into the imperial workforce, expanding trade, improving agriculture, and increasing military size and strength, Emperor Qin greatly increased the power of imperial China. He started construction of the massive wall on China's northern border to block incursions by nomadic invaders, now known as the Great Wall of China.

When Emperor Qin died in 210 BCE, his politically inept son was manipulated on the throne by two of the former emperor's advisers, and all were assassinated in the resulting internecine strife. Popular revolt broke out a few years later, and the weakened empire soon fell to a rival army under Liu Bang, the first emperor of the Han dynasty. Xi'an was renamed Chang'an from the time of the Han dynasty until the Ming dynasty.

The tour group spent the next day visiting the famed Terracotta Army and mausoleum of the Emperor Qin a short distance to the east of Xi'an. The museum guide assigned to the group explained that the Terracotta Army was discovered in 1974 by a group of Chinese archaeologists investigating persistent rumors and clay fragments turned in by local farmers of what was later unearthed as the largest ceramic construct ever found in China. According to an historian writing during the first century BCE, the construction of the necropolis complex involved seven hundred thousand workers. Emperor Qin ordered construction of the necropolis soon after his ascension to the throne at the age of thirteen, and he died thirty-six years later.

The terracotta figures were assembled from cast limbs, torso, and head to be life-sized and held real weapons. The figures were originally painted with lacquer pigments and crafted with individual facial features. The terracotta figures were found in four main burial pits. Pit one, which is about two hundred fifty yards long and seventy yards wide, contained the main army of more than six thousand soldier figures. Pit two contained another two thousand soldiers, one hundred thirty chariots and seven hundred horses. Pit three appeared to be a command post, with high-ranking officers and a war chariot. Pit four was left unfinished by its builders. Many figures in pit one and two were demolished by fire damage and many soldiers were missing weapons, confirming historical reportage of looting and subsequent burning.

The terracotta figures on display were painstakingly reconstructed by archaeologists from fragments of destroyed figures. At one side of the large hall covering the excavation of pit one, Alvin watched as a team of workers sifted rubble to extract ceramic fragments, cleaned them off, and recorded photographs of them marked with identification numbers on computer. Another team was working to re-assemble a warrior figure bit-by-bit from an array of fragments that had been matched together for the one figure. It appeared that about half of the Terracotta Army had been reassembled in the forty years since their discovery.

"The reassembly of the terracotta figures is taking more time than it took to first make them," noted Mr. Tanaka.

"This is grueling work," Alvin said. "It is not simply the reassembly of pieces of the anatomy of a human figure. Each terracotta figure appears to have been uniquely crafted with individual features, and each is wearing scale-armor with hundreds of scales covering each torso. The corresponding pieces of each scale must be re-assembled correctly. So each figure is like a giant puzzle assembled from hundreds of smaller puzzles."

"It's mind-boggling," Jane agreed. "It shows the extreme value the Chinese government places on recovering this priceless cultural treasure of its dynastic history."

"Well, you sound a bit more appreciative of China today than you did yesterday complaining about Chinese public behavior in Guangzhou," Ralph ribbed Jane.

"You've got me there!" Jane laughed chagrined.

Jane's appreciation of things Chinese gained as the tour group that afternoon visited some of the authentic craft guilds in Xi'an for original jade works, jewelry, silk textiles, and Chinese paintings. From the time of the Han dynasty on, Xi'an became renowned as the eastern terminus of the Silk Road. While the designs of goods on sale today reflected modern day tastes, the craftsmanship and artistry lavished on these works were much the same as went into goods traded with the West on the Silk Road two thousand years ago.

That evening the tour group had a fine dinner enjoying some of Xi'an's unique cultural dishes. Xi'an developed a unique cuisine that blended its regional cooking with spices and dishes from Central Asia and from Middle Eastern regions at the western end of the Silk Road. The tour guests tried dishes once enjoyed by Silk Road traders passing through Xi'an, such as *liang pi* "cold skin" noodles, savory cumin lamb burger, and *pao mo* spicy lamb soup. Walking back from dinner to the hotel, they savored the cool pine-scented night air in Xi'an while feeling their bellies warmed within.

Leaving Xi'an the next day, the tour flew to Beijing, the capital of China established during the Ming dynasty in the fourteenth century CE. The Ming pushed out the Mongol khanate of the Yuan dynasty and re-established Han dominance of China over a long and stable reign lasting into the seventeenth century. The third Ming Emperor Zhu Di, considered to be among the greatest of Chinese emperors, constructed the imperial Temple of Heaven and the Forbidden City imperial palace in Beijing, the new capital of the Middle Kingdom. The Ming eventually fell to the Manchu-led Qing dynasty, China's last ruling dynasty before the founding of the People's Republic of China.

Once arrived in Beijing, the tour group started out by visiting the Temple of Heaven. It was renowned for its iconic Hall of Prayer, a magnificent triple-gabled circular building built completely of wood and without nails. It was here that the emperor would come to pray in official ceremonies each year for a good harvest for his people.

Mr. Tanaka noted that the circular shape of the Hall with its peaked cone-shaped roof resembled the shape of the traditional Mongolian tent structure, and the door lintels leading into the Hall were inscribed with Mongol script side-by-side with Chinese script.

"Both scripts say 'May the Everlasting Sky bring good harvests,'" said Latif.

"But why did the Ming builders who ousted the Yuan choose to memorialize them in their most ceremonial of buildings?" asked Mr. Tanaka.

"Isn't that a bit like writing prayers for rapists and rape victims together at the doors to a family planning center?" asked Jane incredulously.

"The Chinese value stability and harmony above all else," laughed Latif. "Writing prayers to heaven both in the script of their dynastic predecessors and in their own was probably meant to bring good luck."

As the tour continued by minibus, the tour guests could see all around Beijing a frenzy of construction of factories, office and apartment buildings. Lines of laborers could be seen at construction sites moving earth and materials or climbing bamboo-laced building scaffolds by the hundreds. The Government was racing for expansion to support living and working needs for the millions of workers moving into the cities from rural areas. Sprawling shanty-towns had hastily grown to house the in-migrating sea of workers from the countryside, hidden behind miles of brightly-decorated temporary walls. Air pollution was becoming increasingly thick, and the Government now had to order industrial plants to shut down one day a week to keep the air from becoming too toxic.

The group next visited the Forbidden City, the Ming imperial palace bordering the south side of Tiananmen Square in the center of Beijing.

"Mao Tse-tung nearly had the Forbidden City razed, but decided it might be used as a government building instead," Latif noted. "However, it was too costly at that time to renovate, so Mao never did anything with it. It was only when Deng Xiaoping wanted to promote tourism for economic development that it was partially restored. Now, the restoration is finally being completed."

The tour group entered through the outer gates into the main courtyard, which was about the size of a soccer stadium and lined with five tiers of inner parapets. The Imperial Hall was made of marble and stood in the center of the complex with a grand front entrance approached by a causeway spanning a moat with five marble bridges. Latif explained the intricate protocol for the emperor receiving official state visits and ministers on imperial business.

"Look how the Hall is covered with bamboo scaffolding crawling with hundreds of masonry workers," noted Mr. Tanaka.

"It reminds me of the human hordes in Guangzhou all over again," said Jane.

"Jane, do you realize that your disgust with China's crowding is just a matter of your viewpoint," Iz said sharply. "You are an American who enjoys having good public services, state-of-the-art medical services, a law-and-order society, and enough personal income to buy anything you may need whenever you may need it. For most in China having those things would be an unimaginable luxury. These workers are happy to have honest work to earn a few *yuan* a day so they can eat a meal, share a tent in a shanty town, and send the rest back home to the family they left behind."

"Well, doesn't it mean that the American system is better than theirs, and they should learn to do things our way," asked Jane, her eyebrows arching in exaggeration.

"No, it does not," replied Iz. "The American system was built by demolishing the lives and plundering the wealth of others, from pushing out native Indians from their lands, to enslavement of blacks to work their plantations, to stripping the West of mineral resources, to indenturing poor, immigrant and child labor in agriculture and industrial sweat shops, to world dominance through ruthless use of military power and technological prowess. That is not a path you would want China and other developing countries to now repeat. You should have more compassion for the struggle the rest of the world faces, and for the mistakes America has already made that it now wants to forget."

"How dare you say that, as an Egyptian who chose to immigrate to America and work for the Defense Department?" Jane countered.

"I am deeply appreciative of what America offers, and for the privilege I enjoy of living and working there, but I never forget what it is like to have grown up poor, to be despised as a foreigner, and to now support a government that threatens and impoverishes others," replied Iz.

"Let's give each other some consideration," Akiko joined in, trying to be a peacemaker. "When we can also see the perspective from another's point of view, then we will be able to understand the whole in a better way, as well as be humble enough to realize that we don't have all the answers."

Jane and Iz were satisfied to leave it at that. Alvin was surprised by the sharpness of Iz's comments on America. However, Latif was relieved to be able to resume the guided tour with everyone's attention.

Behind the Imperial Hall was a massive wall dividing off the imperial family compound. Entering through the gates into the inner courtyard, the inner quadrangle of buildings had a softer atmosphere that reflected the functions of daily life for the imperial family. Latif pointed out that a favorite stop for tourists was the Garden of the Concubines, in which the only living trees on the palace grounds continued to flower.

To one side of the imperial family quadrangle, an imperial museum held some of China's most precious dynastic art treasures saved from looting during China's civil war.

"Look at this artwork from the time of Emperor Zhu Di," Alvin called to Akiko.

"It's beautiful," said Akiko, examining the bronze globe of the Earth embossed with copper plates for the continents and with pearls marking the known cities of the world at that time.

"Its amazing to see how much the Chinese knew about the Earth in the fourteenth century," noted Alvin. "They knew that it was round and rotated around the Sun two centuries before Galileo was punished by the Inquisition for suggesting the same. They clearly knew the extent and position of the North and South American continents between the Pacific and Atlantic Oceans. The Emperor had commissioned his admiral Zheng He to explore the Pacific coast of the Americas seventy years before Columbus mistakenly thought he had arrived in the 'West Indies' by sailing across the Atlantic Ocean."

"This is art exquisitely informed by scientific knowledge," Akiko agreed.

Exiting the Forbidden City back onto Tiananmen Square, the tour group visited the Great Hall of the People, built in 1958 to commemorate the founding of the People's Republic of China. In the Great Mausoleum they saw the embalmed body of Mao lying in state. In the Square itself, the monument called "Progress of the People" showed soldiers, workers and peasants marching together for the glory of Communism. Alvin was reminded that this was the same monument that many students died in front of during the pro-democracy movement that was violently suppressed by the Government.

Later in the afternoon, the tour group stopped to rest their weary feet at the Lotus Garden, a lakeside promenade of restaurants and bars catering to visitors. As they sipped cool drinks in the tranquil setting, the warmth of the waning sunlight of early summer and the muted honking of geese in the lake brought a welcome respite from the long march through China's grand history. They could have been in a quiet corner of any city in the world.

The next morning the tour group departed for Ulan Bataar, the capital of Mongolia, only two hundred miles northwest from Beijing across the Gobi Desert. During the daytime flight, the group could see the unfolding landscape that had been the historic battleground between the Han Chinese and the nomadic tribes of northern Asia. A long-running part of the Great Wall just sixty miles north of Beijing could be seen from the airplane. The Great Wall stretched from the Yellow Sea in the east all along an arc marking the southern edge of Inner Mongolia to China's western border with Kazakhstan, a distance of over two thousand miles. Astronauts on the Apollo 11 mission to the Moon reportedly said it was the only man-made structure on Earth they could see with the naked eye from the Moon.

From the Great Wall northward lay the vast parched expanse of the Gobi Desert, the largest desert in Asia and fifth largest in the world. It covers almost all of the Inner Mongolia region of northwest China and the southern part of the Republic of Mongolia, an independent country after the breakup of the Soviet Union in 1991. At the northern edge of the Gobi Desert is the Mongolian capital of Ulan Bataar. Only fifty miles west was the site of the ancient Mongol capital of Karakorum. The tour group's plane landed in Mongolia on a bright clear day under the Everlasting Blue Sky, revered by the Mongols as the creation spirit of the world.

3

Mongolia: Once Upon the Eve of Destruction

[EXPLORATION LOG: EARTH CE, 116°E, 39°N, 05.30.2013, 10:00:01 AM]

Throughout their history on Earth, modern humans have made killing on a mass scale a primary dominance characteristic of their species. The killing off or subjugation of other hominid species such as Cro-Magnon and Neanderthal was an initial stage of human expansion onto the Eurasian continent. Tribal killing was the next stage of dominance as humans banded together into societies and contended with neighboring ones. This escalated into military killing as societies grew into regional entities governed by supreme rulers in command of organized armies to conduct war against neighboring societies. With the advent of industrial technologies for the mass manufacture of guns, missiles, bombs, and other remote killing weapons, the capability for human genocidal killing evolved to a global scale. Their recent development and proliferation of nuclear weapons has now made global destruction of human societies an instantaneous possibility.

With nuclear-armed forces capable of complete annihilation of populations in an instant, societies have evolved strategies for virtual war management as a defense to accidental engagement in acts of total destruction. This has enabled the citizens of such societies to debate and support virtual war engagement strategies against identified enemies. As societies have advanced, direct killing of the enemy is no longer desirable, as it could incur one's own casualties and is in general "messy" and uncivilized, so killing by use of targeted missiles, robotic drones, and other "smart" mechanized instrumentalities have been adopted.

The combined development of virtual war management with robotic instrumentalities has enabled advanced societies to engage in virtual war gamesmanship or "cold wars" that are largely conducted through communications media of those societies. An occasional surgical strike or mini-intervention may be conducted on the ground where necessary for tactical advantage or to establish credibility for war gamesmanship strategies. The survey needs to investigate whether the conduct of virtual war gamesmanship in advanced societies will lead to increased proliferation and eventual use of nuclear weapons.

The tour minibus pitched and yawed violently as the driver went off-road across the steppe plains leaving the capital Ulan Bataar in the early morning for the historic site of the Mongol capital of Karakorum. The roads in Mongolia were limited and much of them were in bad condition, so tour drivers readily headed off-road when it was the most direct route to a destination. They navigated by driving toward landmarks on the horizon. A valley wall, a rock cliff, a Buddhist *stupa* shrine, or a cluster of traditional round, covered *ger* tents could point the way to a village or a passageway through the surrounding hills.

Latif narrated a brief history of Mongolia, starting with the rise of Mongolian tribal fiefdoms from the first millennium BCE. As a nomadic people sustained primarily by herding livestock, Mongolian horsemen were the mainstay in military conflicts with neighboring kingdoms. The mounted armies of the ancient Xiongnu confederation of tribes in the third century BCE were the greatest threat to the Qin dynasty of China. The Emperor Qin, known for his tomb containing an army of terracotta warriors and war horses, started construction of the Great Wall of China to keep out horse-mounted invaders from

Central Asia. The Xiongnu were later defeated by the Goturks, who were in turn defeated by Uighurs and then by Khitans and Jurchens, continuing the pattern of inter-tribal warfare among the nomadic peoples of Central Asia.

In the late twelfth century CE, the Mongol chieftain Temujin succeeded in uniting the major tribes across Mongolia. In 1206, he took the title Genghis Khan, the Supreme Khan, commanding a united force of some two hundred thousand horse-mounted soldiers. By 1220 he had conquered the Khwarezmian Empire to the west (spanning modern-day Iran, Turkmenistan, Uzbekistan, and southern Kazakhstan) in an especially brutal campaign that ended with the complete annihilation of the cities of Samarkand and Urgench and their populations of about one million each. Genghis Khan died in 1227 during his campaign to subdue the Tanguts of northern China. His family dynasty inherited his armies and continued to wage extensive military campaigns over seventy years expanding the Mongol Empire throughout the Eurasian continent.

Latif pointed out that Mongolia was a landlocked country bordered by Russia to the north, China to the east and south, and Kazakhstan to the west. In this "big sky" country, the plains stretched from horizon to horizon often with nothing but a solitary goat herder or a Buddhist *stupa* shrine as far as the eye could see. Less than one percent of Mongolia is arable land, and the majority of its people have remained nomadic, raising livestock wherever grass and water could be found. The population of Mongolia remains about three million in a land area of half a million square miles, as it was at the time of Genghis Khan. With an average density of just six persons per square mile, Mongolia is the most sparsely populated country in the world.

Due to his foreign affairs writing on arms control, Alvin was aware that the sparseness of Mongolia had another significance beyond what Latif had mentioned. The inhospitable desert lands in western Mongolia had been the early testing grounds for the development of nuclear weapons by Russia and China. At the western border of Mongolia with Russia was the Semipalatinsk test site, and at the southwestern border with China was the Lop Nur test site. Between 1949 and the Soviet signing of the Nuclear Test Ban Treaty with the U.S. in 1989, some five hundred open-air nuclear tests were conducted at Semipalatinsk. At China's Lop Nur test site, about fifty nuclear tests were conducted until China renounced open-air testing in 1996. Nuclear weapons tests since then have been conducted underground.

"Why did Mongolia accept the hundreds of open-air nuclear bomb tests by Russia and China on its borders?" Mr. Tanaka asked Latif.

"It's interesting that you ask that, because Mongolia could have lodged a protest with the United Nations but never did. I think it is in part due to the Mongolians' historical legacy. The Mongols killed tens of millions by wielding their terrifying power of complete annihilation. Much of their slaughter was visited on kingdoms in China and Russia. Perhaps Mongolians admired the development of these modern-day weapons of absolute power. Perhaps the thundering of nuclear tests reminded them how the thundering hooves of the Mongol armies once made all who heard run in fear," said Latif.

"When you understand how simple the physics of nuclear bomb-making are, any country or group that is determined to make nuclear weapons can do so once the necessary fissile material is available. Such material can be reprocessed from fissile byproducts in the spent fuel of nuclear power plants, of which there are some five hundred operating in thirty-one countries, and even more will be needed for the future economic growth of developing countries. The nuclear-armed countries have taught the world that having nuclear weapons is the only thing that makes others fear to attack. Now with the rise of radical Islam, Islamic countries will also want to have nuclear weapons. There seems to be nothing short of war itself that can really stop a country determined to have them," said Iz.

"Why can't we all understand that if more countries have nuclear weapons, then inevitably someone will use them and millions will die," asked Jane incredulously.

"You are asking that because you assume that millions of people dying is a bad thing," observed Iz. "But the Mongols showed that killing millions was tactically the best way to get hundreds of millions to surrender without a fight."

"Yes, fear of annihilation was their strongest weapon," Latif agreed. "This was documented by Tangut historians writing soon after the time of the Mongol conquests. The long-hidden scrolls on The Secret History of the Mongols were finally released by Russian authorities and translated by Chinese historians after the breakup of the Soviet Union. It credits the toughness of the Mongol soldiers from nearly constant tribal warfare, proficiency with their deadly compound bow on horseback, and resourcefulness in mobile warfare and siege tactics as important elements. But the key to their success was their use of psychological tactics. By instilling fear in their enemies by slaughter to the last man, Mongols could demand the surrender of fortified cities without a battle and defeat disheartened armies many times their number.

"If the enemy chose to fight, the Mongols would apply brutal siege methods to force a city into collapse, often by poisoning water supplies and cattle, burning surrounding farmlands, and raining down incendiary matter and infected corpses. When the enemy could fight no more, the Mongols would carry out their promise and slaughter all who remained. Upon command of a black flag raised by a Mongol khan, each warrior had a quota to kill ten of the enemy, making the slaughter of a million people in a day quick work. This enabled fear of the Mongols to spread so that the next enemy they faced would be more likely to surrender. It also had the tactical advantage of leaving no hostile enemy in their rear or burdening the Mongol army with taking prisoners. Mongol psychological tactics instilled fear throughout the world centuries after their power declined." Latif was himself amazed in recounting this history.

"I've read that the number of people killed in the seventy years of Mongol campaigns is estimated at between forty million and sixty million," Alvin told the tour group. "That is about the same number of people as were killed in all of World War II."

"Yes," Latif rejoined, "supposedly ten to twelve million were killed in the crushing of the Khwarezmian Empire in Iran alone. Based on censuses conducted in northern China between 1195 and 1236 CE, the Mongol armies at the height of their conquests killed one out of every three people in their path. The Nazi extermination of Jews was child's play by comparison."

"The Mongols' tactical use of fear of annihilation is not lost on rogue states and terrorist groups today," Iz noted. "Acquiring weapons of mass destruction is only the first stage in their quest for power. Instilling fear among the civilized world about when and where such weapons will be used is the real game to be played."

"I hope for the sake of humanity that you are wrong!" replied Alvin.

"Have you heard the story of the Mongols' Singing Palaces?" asked Lee hesitantly, afraid that his story might be too much for the group. No one seemed to have heard of it, and all looked on expectantly to hear his story.

"Well, on long campaigns, the Mongol soldiers needed to be rewarded with 'rest and recreation' after a victorious conquest. They would round up a thousand women subjects for each *tumen* of ten thousand warriors, one for each squad of ten men. Each woman would be stripped naked with arms and legs tied to stakes in the ground. The men of each squad would come for sex in turn and cast a white stone to the right of a marker if it was a pleasant experience or to the left if it was not. The women were told if a majority of stones were cast to the right they would live, to the left they would be beheaded, and if evenly split they would undergo another round. The women who understood that compliance was a life or death matter quickly learned to sing in their native tongue to soothe the men as they had sex. Mongol records referred to these interludes as the Singing Palaces."

"The Mongols were nothing if not practical," Alvin grimaced.

"Mass rape of women was standard army procedure for subjugated populations, continued Latif. "I read somewhere that the Great Khan had a harem of enslaved women numbering in the thousands, and that as a result of his prolific offspring, one in every twelve men in Asia bears his Y-chromosome genetic imprint."

"Yes, but I've heard that the subjugated women got even," protested Jane. "According to legend, when Genghis Khan defeated the Tanguts in his last campaign, he took a Tangut princess as war booty into his harem. But the Tangut princess concealed a small pair of scissors in her vagina, and wounded him when he came for sex. The legend holds that the Great Khan died of infected bleeding from the severing of his penis. No other account offers a verified explanation for the manner of his death after the Tangut campaign."

"Well, I guess the Great Khan lived by the sword but died by the scissors," laughed Ralph. The group seemed glad for some humor after such gruesome stories.

Arriving at the area thought to have been the site of Karakorum, the tour group looked out on an open field about a thousand yards square that was cordoned off for future excavation. In 1235 after the defeat of the Jin Empire, Genghis's son and successor Ogedei erected a palace at Karakorum as the Mongol capital. From then until the overthrow of the Mongol-established Yuan dynasty in China, Karakorum served as the dynastic storehouse for booty and treasures brought back by the Mongol armies. But the site was long rumored to have been plundered after the fall of the Mongol dynasty. While partial excavations have been conducted, funding for a full excavation of the site has not yet been undertaken.

The Karakorum ruins were adjacent to the Erdene Zuu Buddhist monastery, built in the sixteenth century with the introduction of Tibetan Buddhism into Mongolia. Stones from the ruins of Karakorum were used in its construction. The monastery is surrounded by a high wall capped by one hundred *stupas* around its perimeter and containing sixty-two temples inside. Together Karakorum and the Erdene Zuu monastery form part of the World Heritage Site called the Orkhon Valley Cultural Landscape.

The tour group arrived for a stay of a few days at a nearby Mongolian *ger* tent camp. During the day, the tour group rode on horses and camels trekking through the sand dunes along the adjacent plains. When they returned from their trek, the Mongolian guides held a horse race to entertain the guests. They invited some of the younger men of the tour guests to participate.

"Sorry, I am not an experienced rider and don't want to risk a fall that would end my trip," Alvin declined.

"Well, I'm game," said Iz. "Although it's been a while since I've been in the saddle."

Seven guides, mostly teen-aged boys riding bareback, and Iz on a horse with western saddle lined up at the start. At the crack of a starter's whip, they raced off toward a straw dummy dressed in a traditional *del* calf-length Mongolian greatcoat propped up about one mile away. The Mongolian guides took off so quickly, without any special effort, that it seemed like they were flying on winged horses. Iz seemed to have a decent race start, except the distance between himself and the receding guides widened so quickly that he appeared to be riding backwards. The guides returned in barely two minutes and, as they approached the finish line in a group, tried to pull each other off their horses, laughing all the while. Iz was still on the outbound leg, and when he made the turn and finally finished, he was panting heavily and could not speak for several minutes. The race winner rode over to Iz and gave him a high-five saying "Good race, boss," to which Iz smiled ruefully.

The trek leader came up to Alvin and said, "Next time you come to Mongolia, you ride fast horse, OK?"

"Sure thing!" Alvin chimed back, but he had a new respect for what Mongolians meant by a horse race.

In the cooling air of the waning afternoon, the travelers rested in their tents until dinnertime when they all gathered in a dining tent. Alvin noticed how every bit of the *ger* tent was made of natural materials. The wool tent walls were layered in a cylindrical shape for maximum inner volume on a supporting interior wood lattice structure. The floor was lined with wool carpets woven from goat and sheep hairs.

Two persons could sleep comfortably on opposite sides of a small cast-iron stove in the center, with its obverse sides being used for stowing gear and a foyer for the tent entrance. The two-person capacity was ideal for two warriors in a buddy system, and now for travelers in couples. The stove had a lightweight chimney made of stretched animal gut for exhausting stove gases to an opening in the top of the tent.

The dining tent was of similar construction although of larger size easily accommodating twenty persons in a circle, suitable formerly for two squads of warriors, and now a minibus load of tourists. Latrines were comfortably sheltered in a wool tent over squat trenches dug into the ground. A shower stall was formed by a gut curtain and urn for warmed water suspended overhead on poles. Folding tables and chairs in the dining tent appeared to be the only concession to modernity for the comfort of Western tourists. Like the food eaten by Mongol warriors on the march, cured goat meat and dried vegetables were cooked in a simple stew and seasoned to make a tasty dish. Even though primitive, the whole atmosphere seemed warm and inviting, due in no small part to the simple elegance in the way that natural materials were used.

"Living like this shows that we can live comfortably with far less than seems necessary for a modern lifestyle," Akiko said happily, almost to herself.

The other guests were a bit surprised to hear this comment from a woman who seemed to have all the privileges of an elegant single life. Alvin felt a warm physical attraction for Akiko that he tried not to show. Her smooth soft skin and perfectly coiffed hair and make-up seemed incongruous for a recent widow. She appeared to distance herself from involvement with others, although she was not at all unfriendly or morose. Alvin recalled introducing himself to her, then watched chagrined as she replied with her name, smiled slightly, and turned away. She did the same with the others, and only spoke to Latif to give her cellphone number in case of anything urgent. He wondered why she had chosen to travel with the tour group if she intended to avoid any personal encounters.

"Don't you think it is an essential part of human nature to want to better one's living conditions?" Alvin asked.

He was surprised when she answered with a murmur. "No, it is not essential. We do so when we are bored, or when we can see no meaning in living as we are. There must be a higher purpose that we have for living, other than acquiring better creature comforts, isn't there?"

"And what might that be?" Alvin asked earnestly so as not to sound rude.

"Why, to realize the purpose of living itself!" she answered honestly, trying not to sound enigmatic or obtuse herself.

Alvin was impressed by her delicate but sure manner and evident intelligence. As a happily married man, his mind struggled to maintain control of his suppressed urges. "Yes, but it is hard to remember that when we go through the daily chore of making a living. I am afraid most of us lose sight of it, until perhaps the end."

"One has to learn to live close to the spirit. It is the only way." Akiko demurred.

["Yes, it is the way of life, the way of the Universe."]

The brief conversation with Akiko was ended, but not brusquely, and not without regard for Alvin's feelings. Alvin understood her sincerity, and felt mildly flattered by how she chose to speak to him.

After three days of trekking in the steppes, the tour group returned to city life in Ulan Bataar. It was growing as a modern city of one and a half million, with many young people migrating from rural areas for work in the city. But there remained vestiges of their former nomadic lifestyle everywhere. People from the countryside still preferred to live on small plots of land on the outskirts of town in *ger* tents with a few livestock, rather than in government-subsidized apartments in high-rise buildings. On the streets, many still wore the long wool coats and hats with earflaps characteristic of the countryside. In music and theatre performances, one could see musical instruments and arts and crafts in use today, the same as those dating back to the Mongol period which were on display at the National Museum of Mongolian History.

On the last evening in Mongolia, the tour group went to a touristy dinner show featuring dance and music supposedly of the Mongols. But the performers wore glitzy costumes, and performed dance steps in modern idioms. The music was orchestral and played with modern instruments, and was piped in on an amplified sound system. Yet, despite the beef barbeque dinner and tourist gifts of machine-made scarves and gilded drinking cup souvenirs, the swift movements and zeal of the Mongolian dancers and musicians reminded the tour guests of the iron-willed warriors who once conquered all of the civilized world eight centuries ago.

4

Turkey: Shadow of a New Menace

Through evolution for survival based on quick wits, physical prowess, and use of weapons, humans developed a characteristic will to dominate others, as well as the instinct to avoid domination by others. The human characteristic will to dominance is euphemistically called "free will" by some philosophers. By whatever name, it is a core, species-specific aspect of humans that is deeply embedded in their limbic consciousness. A positive aspect of human free will is a fertile imagination and ability to creatively solve problems for themselves or their society as a whole. A negative aspect of human free will is a perverse stubbornness not to accept what common sense suggests, often to the detriment of themselves and the greater good. The survey will explore whether humans will use their free will positively to solve, or perversely to exacerbate, the problem of nuclear weapons proliferation on Earth.

On the morning of their flight from Ulan Bataar connecting through Beijing and flying direct to Istanbul, the tour had a clear daytime view of the searing expanse of the Taklamakan Desert marking the forbidding boundaries of the Silk Road through Central Asia. This setting for fabled riches, danger, and adventure over the medieval centuries of commerce between Eastern and Western civilizations soon had the guests excitedly regaling each other with their most thrilling travel stories.

As the flight continued west, the dry desert floor began to give way to greener grasslands rising in gradual ascent to the foothills of the Himalayan Range marking the grinding forces of tectonic collision of the Indian subcontinent with Eurasia. As they flew over the highest peaks in the world, Alvin could see mountain goats grazing on the sparse alpine terrain not far below the plane flying at thirty-five thousand feet.

Once over the high Himalayan plateau, the plane flew over a long descent of rocky massifs funneling through the Khyber Pass and opening into the confluence of Asia with Europe known as the Middle East. Latif briefed the tour group with a quick history of the embattled region.

"Following the rise of Bronze Age civilizations in Mesopotamia, great regional empires began to be formed in the Middle East. The first Persian Empire of the Achaemenids arose from about the sixth century BCE to dominate the Middle East, until they were defeated by Alexander the Great. Following his death, reign over his vast conquests was divided up among his former generals. The bulk of his conquests in the Middle East went to Seleucus who expanded control to form the Seleucid Empire. It later declined due to internal conflicts and incursions from Central Asia, and was taken over by the Persian Sassanids in the third century CE.

"In the West the Roman Empire had begun to fragment due to internal corruption and rebellions among its far-flung provinces. Emperor Constantine renamed Byzantium Constantinople and made it the eastern capital of the empire in 326 CE. The western capital of Rome fell in 476 CE to invasion by Gallic tribes, and the ensuing feudal period became known as the Dark Ages.

"With his inspired writing of the Koran, the Prophet Muhammad led an army of zealous adherents in the seventh century CE to seize control of the Arabian Peninsula in the name of Islam. The Islamic conquests were extended by his family and followers throughout the Middle East, including defeating the Sassanids and absorbing Persia as a Muslim caliphate. Islamic Turks in Persia became consolidated under the Seljuks, who forced the Byzantines out of Anatolia by defeat in the Battle of Manzikert in 1071 CE.

"Fleeing from the onslaught of the Mongols in the thirteenth century, migrating Turkic tribes from Central Asia displaced the Seljuks and, with conversion to Islam, took control of their former caliphates. Turkic tribes in Anatolia became united at the start of the eleventh century under Osman Bey, the first ruler of the Ottomans. The Ottomans grew in power and expanded from Anatolia throughout the Middle East. They forced the Byzantines out of Constantinople in 1453, renaming it Istanbul, and made it the new capital of the Ottoman Empire. At its height of power under Suleiman the Magnificent, the Ottoman Empire controlled the Middle East, Central Asia, the Balkans, and North Africa for the next four centuries. But weakened by internal corruption, it aligned with Germany of the Axis Powers and was dismembered by Allied armies in the aftermath of World War I."

The flight had passed over the Salt Desert in northern Iran and was headed toward the eastern border with Turkey. The thick crescent shape of the Caspian Sea was visible to the north. The plane turned to the northwest and flew along the southern shore of the Black Sea bordering Turkey. Latif was energized with obvious delight to tell the tour group a bit of the history of his native country Turkey.

"The Anatolian peninsula is one of the oldest continuously inhabited regions in the world, with Neolithic settlements dating before the tenth millennium BCE. Its language of antiquity was the root from which later Indo-European languages radiated. The oldest name for Anatolia, 'Land of the Hatti,' was found in cuneiform tablets from the time of Sargon the Great in the third millennium BCE. The Indo-European Hittites invaded the Hattians and founded the first major empire in the area from about the eighteenth century BCE. The Hittite rule ended when they were conquered by the Chaldeans from Babylon. A long period of turmoil followed, including incursions by the Greeks at Troy and the western coast of Anatolia in the eleventh century BCE, until the whole of Anatolia was conquered by the Persian Achaemenids in the sixth and fifth centuries BCE and later by the Ottomans, as I mentioned before."

"How was Turkey formed out of the collapsed Ottoman Empire?" asked Lee.

"In the aftermath of World War I, General Kemal Ataturk rallied Turkish forces and forced Greek and Allied forces out of Anatolia, and gained recognition for Turkey as an independent country in the 1923 Treaty of Lausanne. He embarked upon political, economic, and cultural reforms to transform the former Ottoman Anatolia into a modern, secular nation. Turkey was a founding member of the United Nations in 1945, joined NATO in 1952, and is now seeking to join the European Union. With its rising economic power, Turkey has taken on the role of mediating between Western powers and the Islamic world."

"Do you think Turkey's success in the West would be an example for other Islamic countries to follow?" Mr. Tanaka asked.

"Yes, I think the younger generations throughout the Middle East greatly admire Turkey's example," replied Latif.

"But it is exactly for that reason that the older generations fear the modernist secular attitudes in Turkey. With all the turmoil in the Islamic world following the so-called 'Arab Spring,' it would not surprise me if a reactionary group will try to turn Turkey into an Islamic state," offered Iz.

Alvin was surprised at Iz's reply. "But Turkey has been developing as a modern western society for almost a century. It would seem impossible to turn back the clock and have Turkish citizens return to living under Islamic law."

"Oh, I agree that it seems inconceivable now," said Iz. "But look at the ouster of Mubarak from Egypt. It created a power vacuum that many factions are trying to fill. When there are no strong democratic institutions to form a new government that can unite all factions, then the factions can easily devolve into civil war, and the most ruthless one will win. The Muslim Brotherhood has become the strongest faction in Egypt and is preparing to defeat other factions if there is civil war."

"But that would be impossible to imagine in Turkey," protested Alvin.

"No, I think it can easily happen with a sudden shift in events," Iz countered. "Already pressures are building for Turkey's President Erdogan to take a more radical Islamic stance on political and social issues. If Turkey's government becomes more authoritarian and tries to suppress Islamic dissent, it will only invite a more violent reaction. With the Middle East awash in oil money to buy weapons and hire mercenaries, Turkey would be a tempting target for Islamists to expand their global ambitions. All it would take is a spark to set things off." Iz said this as one who had the weight of his own conviction on the subject.

Alvin had worked enough on Middle East foreign policy to know that Iz's scenario was very plausible. He made a mental note to follow up the conversation with Iz later. He was curious what kind of spark Iz thought might set off a "powder keg" in Turkey.

After landing in Istanbul on an afternoon arrival, the tour group checked into their hotel near the famed historic district along the Bosporus, the Golden Horn. For the rest of the day, the tour group was at their leisure to explore the nearby sights of the richness of Istanbul's Ottoman past and its European present.

The next morning the tour group boarded a waiting minibus and departed from Istanbul for a land tour of Turkey. After leaving across the Bosporus Bridge, the minibus motored east on the coastal highway along the southern shore of the Black Sea, then headed south toward Ankara. The tour group stopped for the night in Safranbolu, an ancient town that was an important caravan stop at the western end of the Silk Road. The town was named for its famed blue saffron flower whose aromatic red stigmas were coveted as one of the world's most precious spices.

In the evening Iz invited Alvin to join him at the Old Bath *hamam* in the historic district of Safranbolu. "This is a true pleasure to wash away all your cares and worries about nuclear weapons," Iz laughed.

"It's like a steam bath, isn't it?" asked Alvin.

"Oh no, it's much more. The *hamam* combined the grand architecture of the Roman *thermae* baths with the Turkic tradition of steam bathing and cleansing with water, and was developed to a high cultural form under the Ottomans. It is a uniquely Turkish delight," replied Iz.

"OK, I'm game," Alvin said, wondering what could be so unusual about a steam bath.

From the outside, the bath was a large domed structure with architectural flourishes that seemed more characteristic of a mosque. Upon entering, they were greeted by friendly attendants speaking in muted voices to show them to the dressing rooms and relaxation areas. Undressed and wrapped in towels, they were shown into the main bath. It had a large interior with high vaulted ceilings that were filled with clouds of steam. Cold water rinsing stations tiled in marble with copper fixtures were lined in apses along the perimeter walls. A large marble dais about fifteen feet in diameter occupied the center of the bath. The bath attendants gestured for them to lie down on the dais on their towels.

As they let the steam heat soak into their road-weary bodies, a burly bath attendant wearing a loincloth came in, pointed at Alvin, and set a basin of warm soapy water next to him. As the burly attendant unwrapped a large loofah sponge and stood over him, Alvin suddenly felt woefully naked and at his mercy. The attendant proceeded to scrub down every inch of his body with the loofah sponge wielded like a horse brush. Each arm was lifted and scrubbed, and each leg turned this way and that, with hardly an effort by the attendant. He then flipped Alvin on his back with one arm, and repeated the scrubbing on his front side and face until Alvin nearly cried out in pain. The attendant put the sponge down and proceeded to knead Alvin's soft tissues from his neck to his feet with thick fingers that felt like iron claws. In a few short minutes it was over.

The attendant opened a new sponge and gestured at Iz whose eyes became glazed with fright.

Alvin slowly sat up to a sitting position on the dais panting for breath. He noticed a pool of pinkish brown water at his feet draining toward the bath's gutters and wondered what it could be. In horror he realized it was his dead skin scrubbed off from every inch of his body. His whole body felt strange, like it was a shadow of its former weight and had become transparent and buoyant on the clouds of steam. When the attendant had finished with Iz, they were shown to a rest area outside on a veranda to recline on divans wrapped in towels while sipping tea.

"Wow, now I know why Turkish bath attendants always look like professional wrestlers," said Alvin sheepishly.

"Yes, and ours was surprisingly gentle for such a big man," quipped Iz in jest. He had a wide grin on that said, "Boy, am I happy to find myself alive and unviolated." Together they enjoyed a quiet moment of peace without a care in the world.

The next day the tour group visited the Turkish National Museum in Ankara. The guests were amazed to see artifacts from Anatolian settlements dating back to Neolithic times from more than ten millennia ago. Alvin was especially impressed by the display in one gallery of exquisite examples of Hittite jewelry. One in particular was a necklace made of lapis stones crenellated with garnet and laid out at intervals along a thin woven mesh of gold thread.

"It is absolutely beautiful and unique, isn't it," whispered Akiko behind him.

"Yes, I've never seen anything like it before," said Alvin appreciatively. "It seems as perfect today as it must have been the day it was created."

"A work that can inflame human desire the same five thousand years later can truly be said to be eternal art," murmured Akiko. "Would you like to have lunch together and compare notes on what we liked the best?"

Alvin was floored, and flattered, by the unexpected invitation.

"Yes!" he said, and quickly added, "I've been keeping my list of remarkable things too." He flushed thinking he might have seemed too eager, but Akiko only nodded with a warm, inviting smile. "OK, see you outside the museum after the tour."

Their lunch together was a *pas de deux* of appreciative minds, Alvin for history, and Akiko for art. At the suggestion of Latif to try a Turkish wine from one of the oldest wine-making regions in the world, they shared a bottle of very fine Kavaklidere wine, the best local wine the upscale restaurant chosen by Akiko had to offer. Its mellow earthy taste and slow spreading warmth exactly mirrored the growing affection that seemed to be taking hold between the two.

The tour group woke early the next morning for the drive from Ankara to Cappadocia, a region of stark mountain ranges and alluvial basins populated by tall minaret-like plugs of volcanic ash called "chimneys." Latif as usual had much to relate about the strange landscape they were visiting.

"Cappadocia was part of the central Anatolian Plateau that was occupied by the Hatti people in the late Bronze Age, and later became the homeland of the Hittites. After the fall of the Hittite Empire, it was ruled as a tributary of Darius, the Archaemenid king. After Alexander defeated Darius, Cappadocia was given to his general Eumenes, then later fell to a line of successors until it was taken over as a Roman province.

"Early Christians took refuge in Cappadocia in the diaspora from Jerusalem under Roman repression in the first century CE. They hid in settlements carved into caves, and created exquisite cave churches lined with paintings and frescoes that have been restored by archaeologists. When Cappadocia became a tributary to Seljuk principalities established in Anatolia, much of the population converted to Islam. The Seljuks were later replaced by the Ottomans, and Cappadocia thereafter remained part of the Ottoman Empire until the formation of the state of Turkey. In modern times, Cappadocia has become a tourist destination due to its extraordinary natural formations and historic sites, and is also a center for some of Turkey's finest arts and crafts industries, such as rug making, jewelry, weaving and fine fabrics."

The tour group was invited in the evening to a moonlight cookout followed by a Turkish music performance in a cave auditorium. The event was put on by some of the local merchants who had done well selling their wares to the group. The music performance reached a climax when Ralph brought out his saxophone and jammed with the Turkish musicians, layering his Western jazz riffs on their *Alevi* folk stanzas played on stringed *bagama*. The synthesis of east and west musical styles seemed perfectly natural, even as the tour guests caroused with their Turkish hosts into the late hours.

The next day the tour continued on to the city of Mersin on the southern coast of Turkey on the Mediterranean Sea. Latif recounted that archaeological excavations showed that the coastal area had been settled since the ninth millennium BCE. It was fortified and served as a major Mediterranean port city from the fifth millennium BCE until about the first millennium BCE. The city fell under a series of invaders, then became part of the Roman province of Cilicia and ruled by the Byzantines until it was taken over by the Ottomans.

The group stayed at a coastal inn in Mersin with a spectacular view of the Maiden's Castle, a walled fortress built on an island in Kizkalesi Harbor. That evening they ate dinner at the Blue Dolphin, a small seaside restaurant overlooking the castle which was lit by dramatic floodlighting at night. The guests enjoyed the romantic setting enhanced by lots of Turkish wine and *raki*.

Alvin saw Iz keeping to himself, staring off into the distance. He still relished the pleasurable time they enjoyed together at the *hamam*.

"Penny for your thoughts, Iz?" queried Alvin, a bit hesitant to disturb him.

Iz was silent for a while then answered, "Do you know what is on the other side of the mountains east of this harbor?"

"Hmmm, isn't it a commercial area of Turkey called Adana?"

"Yes," said Iz, "and the home of Incirlik Air Base which is under joint command of Turkey and NATO. Incirlik served as a main hub for U.S. air missions in wars in the Middle East. I've heard that it has storage for some two hundred nuclear bombs that the U.S. shares with its NATO allies."

Iz's answer stunned Alvin. He wondered what possessed Iz to share this information with him. Iz had told him previously that he worked with the U.S. Defense Department on advanced nuclear weapon designs. From his own research work on nuclear arms control, Alvin was very familiar with the "nuclear umbrella" accord under which the U.S. shares its stockpile of nuclear weapons with NATO countries. But he had no idea that two hundred such weapons could be stored just over the hills from where he sat having dinner.

"If your scenario for an Islamist revolution in Turkey were to occur, then it means that these NATO nuclear weapons at Incirlik might fall into Islamists hands," observed Alvin.

"I would say that that is a distinct possibility to consider," replied Iz.

"Chilling thought!" was all Alvin could say, wondering at the unthinkable.

The next day the tour group's itinerary headed west to Konya, the home of the famous Sufi mystic and poet Jalal a-Din Rumi. As a Sufi musician and poet himself, Latif felt a special connection to Rumi and had presented the visit to Konya as a highlight of the Turkey land tour.

"Rumi was born in the early thirteenth century in the province of Balkh in Khorasan, the easternmost province of Persia near the border of Afghanistan with Tajikistan. His father emigrated with the family to the west, fleeing an impending Mongol invasion. After several years, the family settled in Konya, where his father became the head of a *madrassa* religious school. When he died, Rumi inherited his position as *molvi* teaching Islamic religious law and learning Sufism as a disciple of one of his father's students. Late in his life Rumi turned to writing poetry and ascetic Sufi practices.

"Rumi's major work of poetry was the Mathnawi, a six-volume work of some twenty-seven thousand lines considered to be one of the greatest works of mystical poetry in the world. Rumi's other major work was the Divan-i-Kebir written in honor of his spiritual master Shams whom he met late in life. Rumi's central theme, like that of other mystic Sufi poets of Persian literature, was the concept of *tawhid*, the mystical union with the Divine One. Rumi believed passionately in the use of music, poetry, and dance as a path for spiritual awakening. When union with the Perfect One is restored, the seeker can return to life with a greater maturity, to love and to be of service to the whole of creation."

Alvin was impressed by Rumi's devotion to poetry, music, and spiritual awakening and by the universalist viewpoint of the Sufis. He made a mental note of appreciation of Islam as much broader and deeper than he had understood it before.

Latif continued, "Rumi died in 1273 and was buried next to his father in Konya. His shrine became a place of pilgrimage for admirers and spiritual devotees the world over. Following his death, his followers and son Sultan Walad founded the Mevlevi Sufi Order, also known as the Order of the Whirling Dervishes, famous for its trance-like spinning dance. A splendid shrine, called the Green Dome because of its burnished copper roof, was erected over his place of burial. When Turkey became a secular state, state-sponsored religions were banned, and Sufism was de-institutionalized. The shrine of Rumi was then converted to the Mevlana Museum."

The tour group entered the museum through the main gate into a marble-paved courtyard with a marble *sadirvan* fountain. On entering the mausoleum through a silver door, the guests were confronted by a vertical stand of coffins of descendants of the Mevlana family and high-ranking members of the Mevlevi order. The sarcophagus of Rumi was located under the Green Dome, covered with a brocade embroidered in gold with verses from the Koran.

They then entered the adjoining Ritual Hall, where dervishes used to perform the *sema*, the ritual whirling dance of the Mevlevi order to trance music. As illustrated by mannequins, the dervishes kept long beards and wore long black cloaks and strange, rounded top hats, which were said to resemble tombstones representing the Sufi's constant awareness of the temporalness of life. Also on display were specimens of Rumi's Divan-i-Kebir and Mathnawi books of poetry.

Alvin saw in the display one of Rumi's poems entitled "Thirsty Fish," which was rendered in Arabic script and in English. He was impressed by how it ended:

> "This is always how it is
> when I finish a poem:
> A great silence overcomes me,
> and I wonder why I ever thought
> to use language."

["How true. That is why poems are meant to be sung."]

Alvin pondered the enigmatic words of Rumi's poem, but did not know why he felt it resonated so well with him.

That evening the tour group went to a theatre in Konya to see a performance of whirling dervishes and Sufi poetry. Alvin felt his mind go into a trance watching the dervishes surrounded by the centrifugal whirl of their skirts around the steady core marked by their tombstone hats. The where and what of their mystical practice could be explained, but how the Medlevis ever thought of it was a mystery.

The next day the tour continued west from Konya visiting historic places along the way. Stopping in Pamukkale, they visited the ancient hot springs amidst long travertine terraces of carbonate minerals precipitated from the flowing waters.

In Hierapolis near Denizli, they walked through the ancient city given by the Romans to their Pergamon ally Eumenes II in the second century BCE. The walled city was built around hot springs and used as a spa where aristocrats came to soothe their ailments, with many of them staying on to be buried in the necropolis there.

Reaching the Aegean coast of Turkey, the tour visited the ancient temple ruins and hippodrome of Aphrodisias, named after the Greek goddess of love. The city was built near a marble quarry that was extensively used in the Hellenistic and Roman periods, and marble sculpture from Aphrodisias became famous throughout the Roman world.

Driving north along the Aegean Sea coast to modern Izmir, the tour visited Ephesus, a Greco-Roman city built on an ancient settlement site inhabited since Neolithic times. Latif recounted the history of the place.

"This area was first recorded as a settlement named 'Apasa' in Hittite sources dating to the fourteenth century BCE. It became the Attic-Ionian city of Ephesus in the tenth century BCE, and prospered as one of the twelve cities of the Ionian League. It was famed for its Temple of Artemis, one of the Seven Wonders of the ancient world. Ephesus fell to a series of tyrants, to Cyrus the Great of the Achaemenids, then to Alexander the Great and the Seleucids. After being taken over by the Romans, Ephesus prospered and became the second largest city of the Roman Empire after Rome.

"One of the seven early Christian churches among the Gentiles was established in Ephesus. The Bible indicates that the Gospel of John was written here, as well as the letters of Paul to the Ephesians. It was believed that the dying Jesus entrusted the care of his mother Mary to John, and that John brought Mary to Ephesus after the death of Jesus. On a hill above the city, the reputed last home of Mary has been restored in remarkable condition by Turkish authorities. We will stop now for a visit to one of the most important sites of veneration in the Christian world."

"And we should also note," interjected Iz, "that Mary, the mother of Jesus, is revered in Islam as well."

Driving up the steep hill above Ephesus, the tour stopped for a visit to the home of Mary. As Alvin and the tour group walked up the stone-paved pathway, they felt a palpable serenity seeing the small home of layered stone in the shade of the tall eucalyptus trees. A nearby spring bore a marble sign, "*Meryemana Kaynak Suyu*

Icilir," translated as "Mary's Spring Water." Alvin had a moment's inspiration to empty out his bottle of store-bought water and fill it with water from Mary's Spring.

"My wife who is a devout Catholic will be tickled to have this divine water!" he said to Mr. Tanaka, who likewise took some of the sacred water.

"What will she do with it," asked Mr. Tanaka.

"My wife believes holy miracles can happen. Perhaps she might sprinkle some of this water in our garden, so our dying plants can spring to life." Alvin, a lawyer with a scientific background, was not sure if he would believe in a holy miracle even if he saw it with his own eyes.

"Miracles can happen all around you every day, every moment," laughed Mr. Tanaka.

On the morning drive from Izmir to Canakkale, home to the archaeological site of legendary Troy, Alvin sat in the back of the minibus with Iz who seemed in fine spirits.

"I'm really looking forward to touring the site of Troy," said Alvin. "It is amazing that this storied city of Greek and Roman legends actually exists."

"We still hardly know, though, what about Troy was legend and what was fact. For example, did Menelaus actually convince all the Greek states to go to war for ten years across the Aegean Sea because his wife Helen had run off with a Trojan prince?" asked Iz.

"I like to think that the Greeks had political and military reasons for attacking Troy, to gain control of the Aegean coast and the Dardanelles for trade routes to Asia," said Alvin. "The stories of the Judgment of Paris and Helen of Troy were probably created by Homer the Poet to put a romantic and mythological spin on what was basically plunder and greed."

"That sounds about right," laughed Iz.

Latif briefed the tour group on a history of Troy.

"Troy was a major city from as early as the neo-Hittite period, guarding the entrance to the Dardanelle Straits through which sea trade was conducted from the Mediterranean with Central Asia. In Homeric legend, the Trojan War was sparked by the seduction of Helen, wife of Spartan king Menelaus. The Greeks besieged the city for ten years before it was finally sacked after breach of its walls through the famed ruse of the Trojan Horse. Archaeological evidence indicates the likely date of destruction of Troy was 1183 BCE.

"According to Roman legend, when Troy fell the Trojan prince Aeneas fled with other escapees, enduring travails at sea until they landed in Latium in western Italy. There they intermarried with the Latins, beginning with Aeneas's marriage to Lavinia, the daughter of the Latin king. Their descendants Romulus and Remus were reputed to be the founders of Rome in the eighth century BCE. The destroyed Attic people of the East thus became the progenitors of the great civilization of the West, the Romans.

"On the other hand, the Greeks were so depleted from the war that, despite feeble attempts to establish settlements in Asia Minor, they were unable to capitalize on their capture of Troy. Instead they suffered a long period of decline that historians call the 'Greek Dark Ages,' from which they recovered only in the fourth century BCE with the rise of Philip of Macedon and his son Alexander the Great."

"The history of Europe and Asia is like the random brush sweeps of a Jackson Pollock painting," Alvin laughed.

"Well, not so random perhaps. More like the wild back-and-forth swings of a power pendulum driven by plunder and greed," observed Iz.

"And the struggles of East and West continue today. Are we learning anything, making anything better?" mused Alvin.

The tour group checked into a small seaside hotel at the entrance to the Dardanelles. Some guests went for a dip in the clear waters along the front of the hotel, and walked on the seaside boardwalk casting long shadows in the cooling late afternoon sun. A feeling of utmost peace seemed to pervade over all.

In the morning, the tour group crossed the Dardanelles by bridge to a peninsula across from the straits named Cannakale, the site of the bloody engagement known to the West as Gallipoli. There an invasion force of a half million Allied troops were trapped in a siege by a like number of Turkish troops in an ill-fated attempt to gain Allied control of the Dardanelles. Casualties of about a quarter of a million soldiers were sustained on each side over the eight-month campaign, the largest total number of casualties in a single engagement in World War I, and many more died in the disease and squalor of the aftermath. Now, as hallowed ground, the site was preserved as a large parkland memorial. The group took a tour of the small museum, and stopped for a quick lunch on the adjacent terrace overlooking the parkland memorial.

"Perhaps peace is what comes after tragedy ends," thought Alvin, as he looked out over the now-quiet expanse of parkland lined with tall trees that had grown back since the deadly conflict.

5

Istanbul: East Versus West, Again

[EXPLORATION LOG: EARTH CE, 29°E, 40°N, 06.9.2013, 13:00:01 PM]

The average human brain is estimated to contain about one hundred billion neurons interconnected by one hundred trillion synapses. This enables the human brain in theory to distinguish a virtually infinite number of memories, thoughts, or imagined scenarios as distinct entities. While the average human person is conditioned by life's experiences and daily circumstances to operate within a limited set of patterns, each human mind can potentially imagine things that no other human has thought of before. This potential of the human mind for infinite variation leads humans to believe that every person is unique.

Combined with free will, human belief in self-exceptionalism most often biases them to think of their own selves, rather than organizing their thinking for the benefit of their society as a whole. As a result, human actions on behalf of their societies can vary over a wide range depending on their individual personalities, from imagining creative solutions to problems, to devising diabolical ways to destroy others. The survey will explore whether the creative potential of the human mind will be used to solve or exacerbate the problem of nuclear weapons proliferation on Earth.

On returning to Istanbul from their land tour, the tour group had several days for sightseeing in the historic city. The first day they visited the Hagia Sophia church museum in the historic district of the Golden Horn. The Hagia Sophia served as the cathedral of Constantinople until the city fell to the Ottomans in 1453. It was converted by the Ottomans to a mosque and remained so until 1931 when the first Turkish president Ataturk decreed that it be converted to a secular museum of the Republic of Turkey. Famous for its massive dome, it was the epitome of Byzantine architecture and the largest cathedral in the world for nearly a thousand years. True to its name, which means "Holy Wisdom" in Greek, the Hagia Sophia was dedicated to the Logos or Holy Spirit, the third manifest person of the Holy Trinity. It contained a large collection of holy relics and mosaic friezes depicting the incarnation of the Logos in Christ. Alvin noted that the Byzantine emperors depicted in the friezes dated back to the time Christianity first became the official religion of the Roman Empire.

The tour group also visited the Blue Mosque, the paragon of high Ottoman architecture, which was across the way from the Hagia Sophia. Commissioned in 1609 by Sultan Ahmed I after his unsuccessful campaigns in Persia, it was built on the site of the former palace of the Byzantine emperors. The group marveled at the blue-tiled central dome and stained glass mosaics that created an ethereal azure glow that gave the Blue Mosque its name.

The tour group emerged outside the mosque in time to join large crowds of local Turks and tourists gathering in the park across the mosque to hear the call to evening prayers. From there they had a panoramic view of the six minarets encircling the Blue Mosque dome, a distinctive architectural feature recognized the world over. They watched as the mosque and minarets became brilliantly illuminated at dusk by colored floodlights, a sight that left an indelible impression of the evening hour of prayer in Turkey.

The next day the tour guests went sightseeing on their own. Alvin and Akiko headed to the Turkish Arts Museum in search of Attic art and Hittite jewelry. Mr. Tanaka, Ralph and Jane went to the European quarter in the Beyoglu district of Istanbul, visiting streets lined with antique shops, art galleries, music venues, and the Mevlana Museum. Lee Cheng, the Hadleys, and the Merediths took a boat tour to see the sultanate palaces and Roman forts along the Bosporus straits and then went to visit the Grand Bazaar. Opting out from sightseeing, Iz said he would try to meet up with some friends visiting in the city.

After a full morning at the museum, Alvin and Akiko decided to go to lunch at a seaside restaurant that Akiko had read a rave review about. It was in the lively Kumkapi district facing a scenic stretch of the Sea of Marmara. "Be sure to bring your camera," Akiko had suggested. "You might want to get some scenic photos of Istanbul's historic inland sea."

The seaside restaurants of the Kumkapi district were buzzing with lunch patrons sitting outside in the warmth of the noontime sun. The restaurant Akiko had chosen had a lovely view of the sea. She asked for a quiet table outside divided off from the others by some potted plants.

"I'm dying to try the *pazıda levrek*," said Akiko. "I read that it is a Marmarite specialty of sea bass spiced and cooked in chard leaves."

"Sounds very local," Alvin agreed. "I think I'll try some Turkish stuffed mussels and fried *kalamar* squid to compare to Greek and Mediterranean styles of cooking."

They enjoyed a long, slow lunch, with lots of Turkish *raki* to cool their thirst.

While waiting for their desserts of *baklava* and *kadayif*, Akiko asked, looking over Alvin's shoulder, "Isn't that Iz at the corner table inside?"

Alvin glanced over and saw Iz in deep conversation with three men all with heavy beards and appearing to be of Middle Eastern descent. One of them had a very serious expression and sat silent while the others talked.

"They look busy," said Alvin. "Do you want to go over?" he asked, but Akiko shook her head and excused herself to go to the ladies room.

As Alvin sat by himself, he wondered at the odds of Iz having chosen the same seaside restaurant to meet with his friends. As Alvin gazed over between the potted plants, he saw Iz take a black folder out of his backpack and hand it to one of the men. Alvin was astonished as he glimpsed a blue-and-gold seal at the bottom center of the black folder. In his arms control research, Alvin had frequently been given temporary "need-to-know" access to classified CIA documents of the State Department. Such documents were always carried in black folders with the blue-and-gold seal like the one he had just seen. Alvin felt a flush of cold sweat as he tried to think of why Iz might be turning over such a folder to these men.

Remembering his camera, Alvin thought it might be useful to have some pictures of Iz's friends. He slowly reached for the camera in his pocket and moved it under the table to an opening between two branches of the potted plants. He took three photos at intervals when each of the other men's faces was in good view. The man who received the folder had slipped it quietly under the table and appeared to be putting it in a satchel next to where he was sitting. Alvin avoided looking directly at them and positioned his head behind the potted plants as he waited for Akiko to return. Soon Iz and the three men paid their bill in cash and left by a back exit of the restaurant.

"Did you go over to see Iz," Akiko asked when she returned.

"No, our desserts came, and I could not wait to taste them," Alvin replied.

"Oh, such a rude fellow," Akiko laughed.

Alvin smiled back, but inside he was in turmoil over what he had just seen.

As they dallied over dessert, a *muezzin's* call to prayer was broadcast from a nearby mosque. His singing voice was good, a plaintive tenor with melodious articulation. Alvin let the long singsong notes waft over him like a cool breeze restoring a moment of calm to the turmoil he felt within.

"I suppose Iz must feel somewhat at home in a Muslim cultural milieu like Istanbul," said Akiko listening to the call to prayer. "He said he grew up in Cairo and studied physics at Cairo University before being granted a fellowship to do post-graduate work at Edinburgh."

"Yes, he has a very diverse background, doesn't he? I wonder how he divides his loyalties between East and West?" Alvin could not suppress his feelings of suspicion about Iz after seeing him turn over what looked to be U.S. Government classified materials to those suspicious looking men.

"I can empathize with growing up between two cultures," Akiko said. "Growing up in postwar Japan and going to Stanford for postgraduate work in biology, I remember how my classmates in Japan felt sorry for me choosing to attend university in America, while my American classmates looked on me with suspicion even after I applied to become a naturalized citizen. When I married my husband Arnold who was doing Defense work at Livermore Labs, I was subjected to humiliating questioning about my Japanese family for his security clearance."

"May I ask what caused your husband's death?" asked Alvin.

"I still believe his bone cancer was caused by radiation from his work on the x-ray laser at Livermore, but the Government has blocked all my efforts to find out. My husband's death benefits pension included a premium for hazardous work, so that's a concession that his work was hazardous to his health."

Alvin knew all too well how the complex workings of the U.S. Government could become absolutely impenetrable to someone on the outside. He demurred pursuing the subject further. He and Akiko turned their thoughts to enjoying their walk together around the Golden Horn back to the hotel in the sunny afternoon.

Later, with a view of the Bosporus from his hotel room terrace, Alvin tried to think through why Iz, a former Egyptian national doing U.S. Defense research at a government laboratory, might be handing over classified documents to men who appeared to be Muslim nationals.

He recalled that Iz had alluded to his work on computer simulations of advanced nuclear weapons designs, since live testing of nuclear weapons had been banned under the Comprehensive Nuclear Test Ban treaty.

Alvin knew that the physics for producing a nuclear weapon were surprisingly simple and largely accessible to anyone through published information in reference books or on the Internet. Only a small quantity of five to ten kilograms of highly enriched uranium or fissile plutonium is needed to make a nuclear bomb. The basic design for compacting a core of fissionable material by implosion and concentrating neutron release with a tamper of densified material to cause a chain reaction of fissile energy release was developed over a half century ago for the Nagasaki bomb dropped by the United States on Japan to end World War II.

Alvin thought about the possibility that Islamic terrorists might acquire a nuclear weapon on the weapons black market. Strategic nuclear weapons have always been under tight military control. However, smaller field nuclear weapons were deployed by in large numbers in the 1960s and 1970s by both NATO and the Soviet Union for defense against massed tank attacks. They were later withdrawn under the SALT treaties because they were deemed too likely to be used. Such field warheads were small enough to be fired from a portable launcher, some weighing only about fifty pounds and as small as one foot in diameter. Some Soviet field nuclear weapons withdrawn after the breakup were rumored to be unaccounted for, and it was possible that one or more could have been diverted to the weapons black market.

After the killing of Al-Qaeda's leader Osama bin Laden by a U.S. special-operations team, Islamic media reports had noted rumors about a "big strike" his successor Ayman al-Zawahiri was planning to avenge bin Laden's death. Zawahiri studied medicine at Cairo University where he became radicalized by Islamist politics promoted by the Muslim Brotherhood. He became the founder of Islamic Jihad in Egypt and orchestrated its merger with Al-Qaeda in 1998. The media reports also mentioned rumors of a nuclear weapon Al-Qaeda might have acquired from arms dealers following the breakup of the Soviet Union.

Alvin thought about a likely scenario for Al-Qaeda to acquire and use a field nuclear weapon. Al-Qaeda was known to have high-level contacts with Pakistani nuclear scientists reputed to have transferred nuclear weapons knowledge to Iran, North Korea and others. If Al-Qaeda had gotten control of a field nuclear weapon, it would be inclined to use it on a target near former zones of Soviet occupation in Eastern Europe or Asia Minor, since it would be too risky to try to move the bomb abroad through ports and checkpoints into Europe, the U.S., or an allied country.

Turkey is a major transit center for Muslim nationals and could be a likely location for Al-Qaeda to hide a stolen field nuclear weapon. Striking a U.S. or NATO military target in Turkey might be popular with the "Muslim street" and could drive a wedge between Turkey and its NATO allies.

Field nuclear warheads were known as "enhanced radiation, suppressed blast" weapons designed to have an intense radiation zone and limited blast radius suitable for use against massed tank columns. Such a weapon would be ideal for use against a U.S. or NATO military base. It would minimize nearby civilian casualties so as not to turn popular opinion against its users. But which U.S. or NATO target in Turkey?

Alvin nearly fell over feeling faint. It all came together for him in a flash. He remembered the conversation he had with Iz about the Incirlik Airbase storing some two hundred nuclear bombs that the U.S. shares with its NATO allies. The Incirlik Airbase is located far from Turkish civilian communities. A small field nuclear weapon could have a reduced blast zone limited to the base, and might leave some of the storage bunkers for NATO nuclear weapons on the base intact. Other than Turkish Air Force personnel on the base, no Muslim civilian deaths would need to be incurred.

Besides wiping out all NATO personnel and eradicating an important Western military facility, an enhanced-radiation bomb attack on Icirlik Airbase would afford Al-Qaeda an opportunity to capture some of the two hundred NATO nuclear weapons stored there. Irradiation of the base would not deter Al-Qaeda suicide martyrs from entering right after the blast to try to remove the stored nuclear weapons. The weapons could be loaded on small, unregistered aircraft landing at the airbase then flown to dispersed locations of Al-Qaeda cells, such as in Afghanistan, Pakistan, Yemen, and Somalia.

With stolen nuclear weapons under its control and dispersed among host cells, Al-Qaeda would become a nuclear-armed hegemon for radical Islamism to be reckoned with. The moderate Turkish government may be pressured by Islamist popular opinion to cater to the new nuclear-armed power. Accession to the EU would be of the question, and Turkey could then easily devolve into an Islamist state. Alvin broke out in a cold sweat as he recognized how the expanding consequences of such an attack could lead to spectacular strategic success for Al-Qaeda far beyond imagining.

Alvin knew that the key to having a viable enhanced-radiation bomb was to maintain its tritium-deuterium charge used as a trigger for boosting neutron release into fissile fuel. The tritium is charged to undergo fusion with deuterium into helium releasing high-energy neutrons. The free neutrons can activate fission fuel targets in a chain reaction, so that both fission and fusion can escalate in parallel. This greatly increases the energy yield from a small amount of fission fuel.

However, tritium is an unstable isotope and undergoes continual radioactive decay. So it would be necessary to replenish tritium in the trigger of an enhanced-radiation bomb periodically. The estimated tritium charge for a small warhead of twenty-kiloton yield would be only about four grams or, with a half-life of twelve years, only about one-sixth of a gram of tritium per year to keep the trigger for such a warhead viable.

Tritium can be produced in nuclear reactors by activation of lithium-6 in fuel rods or heavy water with deuterium. Fresh tritium could be obtained by reprocessing irradiated byproducts in spent fuel from a clandestine reactor in a non-NPT country such as

Pakistan or North Korea. Alvin recalled that the optimal delivery design for recharging tritium into an enhanced-radiation weapon had been a matter of considerable weapons design debate. But with the comprehensive ban on testing of nuclear weapons, tritium recharging in enhanced-radiation weapons could only be designed by computer simulation in compliance with the treaties.

Alvin suddenly realized the possible significance of Iz's meeting with the men in the restaurant. Iz had mentioned that his work involved computer simulations of advanced nuclear weapons, which could have included tritium recharge delivery in enhanced-radiation weapons. The blood rushing in quickening pulses in Alvin's head sounded like the rumblings of distant thunder.

After dinner that evening, Alvin spotted Iz having a drink by himself at the hotel bar and joined him.

"Hi, how was your day touring?" asked Alvin.

"Oh, I went walking in the historic district around our hotel. It reminded me a lot of some of my old Cairo neighborhoods, although the Turkish language is completely different."

"Akiko and I had lunch in Kumkapi by the water and thought we saw you with a group of men in the restaurant."

"Oh, yes," said Iz slowly, "I met some Istanbul contacts introduced by a friend for lunch. They are computer programmers working here in the city."

"Did you find anything in common? They must not do the kind of work you do," Alvin replied, registering Iz's slight twitch with a side glance.

"Yeah, actually they are working on a math applet for an Internet music recommender program using the same programming APIs as I use in my physics research," said Iz as his gaze steadily met Alvin's.

Alvin did not know enough about programming of mathematical algorithms to be able to respond knowledgeably. He hesitated with a comeback, and decided to take a risk. He forced a chuckle to break the ice, "I thought I saw you hand them an envelope that looked remarkably like State Department envelopes I get when I receive classified material."

Iz gave a deep laugh, which was paced slower and went on a split second longer than seemed natural. "Oh, that. Yes, I like to keep those envelopes sometimes when I get them at the office to impress my daughter with the 'important' work I do."

"But you know as well as I do that State Department policy requires that all courier envelopes used with classified documents be tracked and returned to its originator," Alvin replied testily.

"Yes," said Iz without missing a beat, "but you know too that some documents are sent one way to be retained for a while by the recipient. I just like to keep some of those envelopes around because their gold seal looks so cool."

"And so you decided to use it to hand documents to people in a foreign city that you have never met before?" Alvin asked incredulously, amazed at the thinness of Iz's deception.

"Oh, I've met with Mr. Alshaz and Mr. Hammad online before. They are quite the pranksters, always pulling my leg. We have been corresponding about a simulation technique for updating a music recommender program using cluster analysis of data patterns. The simulation technique shows what happens when old music preferences are exhausted from the system and new music preferences are injected in. But what I shared with them has nothing to do with my Defense research."

Iz's expression was sincere and not hostile. He seemed content with his response and did not invite any further exchange. Alvin recalled that the stern faces of the men meeting with Iz had seemed anything but fun.

Akiko appeared suddenly at the bar and took a seat next to them. "Hey, anyone want to buy a lady a drink? It's tough to get male attention in here," she said winking at Alvin. Alvin grinned and let go of his questioning of Iz.

"Your smallest wish is my mortal command, Bathsheba. What is your pleasure?"

"Kangaroo with a twist of lime, please. Suitably biblical?" Alvin

74

felt flattered by Akiko's way of looking at him in a level way without any implication, yet made him feel a deep attraction.

Iz let out a yawn and excused himself. "Sorry to turn in early, but I want to get a good night's sleep for tomorrow's early flight to Edinburgh."

"Well, a busy man must know when to call it a day," quipped Alvin, turning to Akiko for friendly conversation. In the back of his mind though, he felt only dread about his interaction with Iz.

"Man feels dread not knowing which is better to keep:
What he has now, or what he might save later
When suffering by all may be many times greater,
Becoming a black hole of loss endlessly deep.
The solution for mankind is to fool his skeptical mind
To think more now is greater than Earth can bind,
Then he might act today feeling the end is near,
Far better than to wait too late to see what all fear."

6

Edinburgh: From Enlightenment to God Particle

[EXPLORATION LOG: EARTH CE, 4°W,
51°N, 06.14.2013, 3:00:01 PM]

Humans have a mental characteristic I will call "fecklessness." By that I mean not just do-nothing or irresponsibility, but rather the tendency to make more trouble or cause more of a mess by what they neglect to do than create any good by what they choose to do. It is the human analogy to the physical Second Law of Thermodynamics that entropy in any discrete system will increase over time, so that the system dissipates toward greater disorder until maximum equilibrium is reached. Humans seem predisposed toward fecklessness because everyone carries some kind of personal grievance from their past leading to a feeling that "I want payback," and to a surprising degree the daily actions of humans are subconsciously dictated by that sense of grievance.

A person's sense of grievance may arise simply from birth trauma, or having a "bad childhood" or "feeling deprived," or at the opposite end of the spectrum, it may arise from a long history of a people's being oppressed or marginalized. On a personal level, it can be manifested in a person not doing the many daily acts of personal responsibility that would keep society safe and clean for all. On a societal level, citizens may lobby loudly for their own causes, even though their demands for disproportionate benefits may undermine the economy for all. In political discourse, everyone says that they want to leave Earth a better place for their children than they found it, yet their actions tolerate, if not promote, excessive consumption, waste, and resource depletion. In foreign relations, one nation may attack another and not realize that the death and destruction they cause may require hugely unsustainable costs of ongoing occupation, nation rebuilding, reparations, or simply the blood hatred of the victims for centuries to come.

Human fecklessness can be corrected by shifting the focus of one's attention from doing good for one's self to doing good for all. This requires a person to take a viewpoint with a higher consciousness of life on Earth to see what all can share in living peaceably and righteously with the whole. While entropy will inevitably increase, peaceful and righteous sharing with all could perpetuate a better life on Earth for a much longer time. The survey will explore whether humans can shift their minds from fecklessness toward a higher consciousness of life on Earth.

The tour group departed from Istanbul flying west to Edinburgh, their next destination across Europe on the east coast of Scotland. It was a magnificent day under a clear blue sky to be flying over Europe, thought Alvin. From his window he could see the Black Sea's expanse northward to Russia as the plane climbed to cruising altitude. He recognized a broad river of deep blue water meandering to the west as the beloved Danube of European song and literature. As the flight flew west, Alvin could trace the river from its wide-mouthed delta on the Black Sea, through the forested expanse of the Hungarian steppes, through Austria and the Black Forest of Germany, and finally to its origins in the Alps in Switzerland.

Latif gave the tour group a brief history of the rise of European nations to become world powers in the seventeenth century to the present. "It started with fresh currents of intellectual and philosophical thought that coursed through Europe in the Age of Enlightenment, using the power of human reason to throw off the Dark Ages of feudalism, intolerance and suppression. A new generation of European thinkers, such as Spinoza, Locke, Newton, Descartes, Rousseau and Voltaire, woke up a moribund Continent, using the invention of the printing press to rapidly disseminate their newfound knowledge and ideas.

"The Enlightenment's new conception of mankind's place in the world led to wholesale reform of European states toward more progressive governments and the unleashing of private initiative to bring about rapid industrialization. The spreading dynamism fueled the colonial expansion of European states around the world, using their rising superiority in industrial might and military power to extract riches, materials, and cheap labor from colonies abroad.

"Great Britain arose as the greatest colonial power of Europe, eventually spanning every continent with its imperial domains. Merging the kingdoms of England and Scotland in the Treaty of Union of 1707, and later Ireland in 1800, the united Great Britain under its newly formed Parliament adopted comprehensive industrial policies that put its legions of former subjects to work in coal mines, factories, and public works, and in its colonial enterprises and armies around the world. Great Britain quickly overtook Spain and Portugal in claiming vast new realms of colonial wealth. The loss of its American colonies in 1789 following a war of independence turned British ambitions farther afield to Africa, the Pacific, Asia and India. Following the defeat of Napoleonic France in 1815, Great Britain enjoyed nearly a century of dominance as the largest and most powerful empire in the world."

Latif explained that the itinerary for the European leg of the tour had bypassed the usual tourist centers of Athens, Vienna, Rome, Munich, and Paris, and instead chose Edinburgh for its major role in the Age of Enlightenment and the rise of Great Britain as the new global power of the West. In particular, its great University became the center of confluence for some of the major intellectual figures of that time, including naturalist Charles Darwin, physicist James Clerk Maxwell, philosopher David Hume, mathematician Thomas Bayes, political economist Adam Smith, surgeon Joseph Lister, and inventor Alexander Graham Bell. As the tour's flight flew over the

English Channel to the aggregate of lands known as the British Isles, it was a visual reminder of the uniqueness of this mighty archipelago from continental Europe.

On arrival in Edinburgh, the tour group checked into their hotel, a classic edifice near the top of the Royal Mile that enjoyed a superb view of Edinburgh Castle. The fortified castle was built on Castle Rock, a solid basalt plug of an extinct volcano rising two hundred fifty feet above the surrounding plain, which tapered to a glacier-eroded tail to the east that formed the only accessible route to the castle and on which the historic buildings forming the Royal Mile were built. To the tour visitors, the castle appeared to be an impregnable fortress. Latif recounted its history of nearly constant sieges, captures, and recaptures from the time it was built under Scottish King Malcolm III in 1093 until Sir Walter Scott recovered the Crown of Scotland and decommissioned the castle to a historical site in 1818.

That night the tour group was treated to the unearthly sounds of bagpipe and drum bands of the Royal Edinburgh Military Tattoo in the esplanade at the entrance to Edinburgh Castle. The Tattoo is held annually in honor of the service of Scottish soldiers in the British armed forces. The sounds of bagpipes and drums had been the signature martial music for British imperial forces around the world. The tour guests had a great view of the Tattoo performance from their hotel rooftop. Alvin felt the hairs in his skin prickle as two hundred bagpipes of invited bands from the Commonwealth of nations massed in the opening performance and filled the air with a skirling wall of sound.

"Ah, it sounds like a call to glorious war, doesn't it?" quipped Iz, obviously enjoying the performance.

"It is certainly a mystery how air from an underarm bag sent through a reed pipe creates just the sound that will stir men to fight to death for their country," replied Alvin.

Akiko joined in, "Perhaps the male Y-chromosome has a gene that causes a tiny auditory hair in the ear to stimulate the brain to a fighting response."

Alvin thought this was a good guess since bagpipes seemed to provoke that response only in males.

"In contrast I've read that hypothalamus stimulation produces a 'tend and befriend' response in women," Akiko continued. "The auditory stimulus of the cry 'mama' from babies has been found to generate a lactating response in female breasts from oxytocin released by the pituitary gland."

Alvin tried hard to focus on the scientific facts and avoid a craven response to Akiko's analogy. From a side glance, Alvin caught a knowing wink from Iz and decided that they shared the same typical male response.

Bright and early the next morning, the tour visited some of the historic buildings along the Royal Mile. From the Edinburgh Castle at one end, they toured the National Library, St. Giles Cathedral, the Old Parliament House, to the Palace at Holyroodhouse at the opposite end. The Palace was the official residence of the Queen in Scotland, and is used by the Royal Family for official state ceremonies and entertaining. Akiko and Alvin took in every detail of the Royal Apartments, which were renowned for their exquisite plasterwork and ceilings, royal furnishings, and incomparable collection of Brussels tapestries.

On the return walk, the tour group had reserved an early dinner at the famed Balmoral Hotel at the foot of Northbridge and Princes Streets. The Balmoral's majestic clock tower was an Edinburgh landmark visible from all around. The guests were thrilled by the hotel's luxurious halls and furnishings, and ecstatic to be seated in the famed restaurant Number One that had earned its Michelin star for the umpteenth consecutive year. The tasting menu that night was a special seasonal creation of its executive chef, featuring the finest and freshest Scottish produce and wild game paired with fine wines from all over the world.

Served at a long table for the tour group, their dinner started with an *amuse bouche* of fresh Scottish smoked salmon and roe, followed by a Strasbourg *foie gras*, and a wonderful chilled artichoke soup intervened. The first main course was a poached Atlantic halibut with dill and *beurre blanc* sauce. It was followed by a very tender rack of Highland spring lamb in sauce *Soubise* of leek and wild heather honey. The dinner ended with a selection of Scottish cheeses, including a Tobermory cheddar, Maisie's Kebbuck cow's milk cheese, creamy Dunsyre Blue, Lanark white cheese, and Clava organic Scottish brie. Alvin relished topping off the tasting with a rare Bruddladich 20-year single malt scotch aged in a Chateau d'Yquem sauterne cask.

On the walk back to the hotel, Alvin accompanied a purring Akiko, who recounted each dish of the menu under a spell from the exquisite tasting. "Clearly, the best meal of the trip, and the best tasting menu I have ever had."

The sky was lit by a hazy albedo of nightime lights of Edinburgh's historic buildings. Soon it turned white as a thick mist blanketed the building spires, and a heavy rain began to pour. Alvin and Akiko were caught in the rain with only Alvin's small travel umbrella between them. He supported Akiko as they dashed for cover in the corner of a tall stone building. Breathlessly, they huddled with their backs to the corner walls under the umbrella's small circle of cover from the rain.

Alvin felt the soft smooth curves of Akiko's body pressed alongside his. He inhaled the sweet scent of her damp hair, which reminded him of the scent of *puakenekene* blossoms in the forests of Hawaii.

"This rain has brought us close together in the best of circumstances, no matter the damp," he said softly.

Akiko did not resist his taking a small initiative. She snuggled her body closer to his, letting him know that she was enjoying the moment as much as he was.

"Can we be as intimate as we are this moment, without feeling a loss for those whom we hold dear?" Alvin asked, more to himself.

"I have often wondered if I could be intimate with another man after my dear husband died. I know now how good it feels to be spiritually intimate with another, even if I could not allow myself to be physically intimate without remorse. I cherish this moment as being perfect as it is. Do you understand?"

"Yes, I do," replied Alvin, surprised at himself since he had always before had the male viewpoint that the only true intimacy with a woman needs to be consummated by having sex. This spiritual intimacy was new to him, and he felt blessed to have this moment. They snuggled closer, and together became as one, attuned to the symphony of the rain on the pavement stones.

The next day the tour group visited Edinburgh's Old Town, home to the University of Edinburgh. Latif recounted that the university was founded in 1583 by edict of King James VI as a public research university. It became the intellectual center of Great Britain during its imperial era. Some of the greatest intellectual minds of the West once taught eager and ambitious students lucky to be invited within its hallowed, ivy-covered walls.

Iz was beside himself with delight. "It's great to be back on this campus again. This is where I came to do my doctorate after transferring from University of Cairo. I remember this place for its wonderful atmosphere of learning and collegiality. They had some of the most prominent professors in the world here, and they were all so approachable and gracious with their time that we students felt truly privileged to be among them."

"What research did you do here?" asked Alvin.

"Theoretical physics in the late eighties. My research advisor was the great Peter Higgs, known for his grand synthesis in quantum electroweak theory."

"Do you mean your research advisor was THE Higgs whose name was lent to the Higgs boson, commonly known as the God Particle?" Alvin was astonished.

"Yep, one and the same. His work centered on how subatomic particles acquired mass after the Big Bang. Higgs proposed that they acquired mass as a result of interacting with a force-inducing field permeating space known as the Higgs Field. Interaction with this field is represented by a particle referred to as the Higgs boson, which has been validated in experiments at the Large Hadron Collider at CERN. This validates the Standard Model of particle physics as a scientifically correct description based on quantum mechanics.

"How did the Higgs boson come to be known as the God Particle?" asked Alvin.

"The coining of that nickname is attributed to his colleague Leon Lederman who originally intended to call it 'the goddamn particle' because of its elusiveness in being found, but changed it to 'the God particle' to avoid scandalizing media coverage. As an atheist, Higgs was not pleased to have the particle central to his field theory nicknamed in media stories as the God Particle," Iz noted.

"Now that experiments at the Large Hadron Collider have confirmed the existence of the Higgs boson, I guess that Peter Higgs and the other authors of the Higgs Field theory will be awarded the Nobel Prize. That will be his opportunity to disclaim the God particle name and remind the world that they can now refer to it correctly only as the Higgs boson," laughed Iz.

Having studied physics at the college level, Alvin was impressed to learn that Iz's depth of knowledge went to the very frontiers of particle research in theoretical physics. But he could not get out of his mind what he had seen at the restaurant in Istanbul that Iz might do with that knowledge.

After dinner that evening, Alvin saw Iz in the hotel lounge and came over to join him. They ordered drams of portwood-finished Mortlach single malt scotch that Iz had found as a favorite years ago during his time in Edinburgh. With the amber *uiskeag* "water of life" slowly spreading warmth within, the two men settled down to a conversation both knew they would need to have.

"So what was the great Peter Higgs like as your professor?" Alvin asked to start the conversation.

"Oh, he was just a joy to learn from," said Iz. "He could explain things in a simple and direct way that made otherwise baffling concepts seem natural. As you can appreciate, this is a hard thing to do in quantum physics."

"Yes," Alvin chuckled, "I remember when my daughter was five years old and asked me, 'Daddy, why do the stars shine?' I tried my best to give an explanation of general relativity suitable for her age, but when I got to the process of nuclear fusion from lighter to denser elements in a star's core and saw her horrified look, I knew I would fail as a physics teacher."

"Hah, I bet you scorched her young mind for good!" laughed Iz.

"Yes, she never asked me a science question again, and she has claimed only to like reading about science by herself. How about you, can you explain to your daughter what it is you do?" asked Alvin, shifting the topic in Iz's direction.

"Well, I tell her daddy uses a computer to find new ways to make things go boom! I think maybe that is why she seems to like things like fireworks, Mentos dropped in diet Coke, nerf guns, you know. Fortunately, she thinks I'm having fun at work, like designing a jack-in-the-box, not weapons."

"How about yourself? How do you feel about your work designing weapons of the most catastrophic sort?" Alvin wondered if Iz would reveal his true feelings.

"Well, discovering secrets to making nuclear weapons definitely has been a huge technological development for mankind. We cannot disavow the knowledge that we have gained: it is here to stay. We can only try to become wiser and stable enough to control our use of this knowledge. What I work on develops knowledge of how these weapons can be made and used, and therefore informs our government and global monitoring agencies of ways in which such weapons should be monitored and controlled." Iz seemed very sincere as he said this.

"Well, global monitoring under the Non-Proliferation Treaty does not seem to be working. Iran is a signatory to the NPT, yet it seems they have found ways to circumvent the treaty and continue their development of nuclear weapons. How can Iran be stopped? And North Korea, which signed the NPT, has since withdrawn from it and has declared that it will conduct further nuclear tests. How can it be stopped?" asked Alvin.

"Practically speaking, Iran cannot be stopped from developing nuclear weapons if they are determined to have them, unless you are prepared to ignite a war in the whole Middle East. The Iranian people feel entitled to pursue weapons development for their own security. Economic sanctions ultimately won't work since Iran has lots of oil. It can also hold the Persian Gulf hostage in the event of a strike against their nuclear facilities. In contrast Israel has had nuclear weapons since 1968 and the West has had little to say about that. North Korea probably does feel threatened by the U.S. and South Korea with which they are still technically at war. Developing nuclear weapons has given North Korea the leverage it feels it must have to hold the U.S. at bay. In both cases, the West will have to bide its time and try to stay one step ahead of the game of deterrence. It is a very deadly chess match, and whether the end game will be checkmate or stalemate, no one can be sure," Iz said, more to himself.

"Practically speaking, that seems correct," countered Alvin. "But tolerating weapons proliferation to avoid war now only seems to put mankind at greater risk that someone will use those weapons later for whatever compelling reasons they may have."

"Yes, that's true," Iz replied. "But man's nature toward dominance always wants more effective weapons to ensure one's own survival. Our best hope is to act tactfully to discourage any new proliferation, while we develop effective defenses to the use of these weapons and to implement effective responses to any threatened use. In this way, we can provide ongoing assurance to others possessing or seeking nuclear arms that we are not threatening our use of them, even as we provide assurance to ourselves that we have an effective response if we are threatened."

Thinking it over later, Alvin had to agree with Iz's point of view, which seemed genuine and not tainted by any agenda to leak nuclear secrets to a hostile party. He had reached a dead end with trying to assess Iz's inner motives, and had no choice but to let things go. What he had seen in the restaurant in Istanbul may have in fact been a harmless sharing of an Internet music recommender program among web friends, as Iz maintained. If it was not, then Iz would not likely admit anything further.

As Iz had opened his eyes to the possibility, Alvin decided he would write an article for immediate submission to his former editor at *Arms Control Journal* on a hypothetical scenario of Al-Qaeda acquiring a field nuclear weapon and needing to obtain information on how to recharge its tritium trigger. Such an article may be useful to alert IAEA and NPT monitoring agencies to a possible proliferation scenario that they might not have considered before. The vulnerability of NATO nuclear weapons bases to an enhanced-radiation bomb attack, and the political consequences of such an event occurring in an Islamic country like Turkey might provide a new spin on deterrence thinking. The further possibility that multiple live nuclear weapons might be stolen from a disabled base and dispersed to Al-Qaeda cells in rogue countries could pose a new strategic arms threat of unprecedented magnitude, for which suitable safeguards might not yet have been considered or deterrence measures devised. Alvin felt convinced that, given recent developments, the timing was right to write such an article now.

The next day was a free day for the tour, and several of the guests got together for a golf outing. Don Overton had found a group of public golf courses called Edinburgh Leisure, which offered a choice of golf venues with great views within the city without having to be a member and for very reasonable rates. "You can't beat green fees of $25 and no waiting to golf right in the city of Edinburgh." For the group's outing, he reserved at the parkland Silverknowes Golf Course on the outskirts of the city overlooking the River Forth. Lee, Mr. Tanaka, and the Hadleys joined the Overtons for the golf outing, while Ralph and Jane had a music conference to attend. Akiko decided she would go shopping at the fine stores on the Royal Mile.

Alvin was very tempted to join the golfing but he had decided to spend the open day working on his article on the hypothetical scenario of Al-Qaeda's acquiring and arming an old Soviet field nuclear weapon. Alvin intended to submit the article before he left Edinburgh, so that by the time the tour group visited their next stop in New York City, he could discuss it with his former editor for publication in the next issue of *Arms Control Journal*. Alvin knew he had no time to waste, much as he wanted to enjoy a fine round of golf in historic Edinburgh.

After a full day for everyone, the tour guests went to The Last Drop, a landmark Edinburgh pub on Grassmarket, for some good pub food, then later to a nearby spot for a *ceilidh* performance of traditional music and song. As the tour guests settled into their seats around an open table at the back, an instrumental group started playing Gaelic music on fiddle, flute, accordion, and *bodhrán* drum.

With the music setting a lively beat, people in the audience got up to dance, with everyone immediately queueing up in a set dance of four couples each to a square. In turn each couple changed positions with the facing couple, then facing couples changed partners with each other, while keeping step to the music. Another kind of traditional dance was performed with the women dancing steps in an inner ring while the men came to each in turn along an outer ring.

Alvin could not resist the moment. "Would you like to dance?" he asked Akiko.

"Yes, I'd love to," she blushed, her eyes shining.

They had no hesitation as novices taking their places on the dance floor, as it seemed participants of any skill were welcome. The night wound on in cheery dance and lively music into the wee hours.

"Lads, step lively to the music of the fiddler,
Ladies, give grace to your partners' embrace,
Let all be enthralled in breathless spell,
As time recedes before the fiddle's fervor.
What more could one ever want than this,
Dancing in timeless, swaying bliss?
This ecstasy fulfills all one can wish for,
To receive the blessing life has in store."

7

Barcelona: Hope is
Our Sacred Family

[EXPLORATION LOG: EARTH CE, 3ºE,
42ºN, 06.18.2013, 1:00:01 PM]

Humans tend to identify their personal selves with their bodies. This is because a body and its supported brain are needed to carry on physical functions and provide physical awareness for the individual human being. Life forms on Earth evolved by the first three billion years from cellular to multicellular to organic hosts for multiply reproducing parts such as fungi, sponges, and coral. Eventually, host-bound organisms evolved with complete organic functions required for an individual polyp to live on its own, and the complete organism developed the capability to detach from the host and live and reproduce as a separate organism. Continued evolution brought about the development of sexual types and sexual reproduction which differentiated the genetic pooling of traits so that natural selection of the fittest to survive led to perfection in expression of species as well as to differentiation of species. Most lower life forms that became individuated have retained some relatedness of individual organisms to hosts of their species, such as fungi growing in circles, insects organized in colonies, fish aggregated in schools, or birds flying in flocks. However, humans with their high degree of self-awareness and free will have retained very little relatedness as part of a larger society, much less as part of the human species on Earth.

Humans have a need to remind themselves that they are part of a greater whole of human species. At a personal level, they will often bond through love and/or marriage to a mate or partner, identify with a family and/or larger community, and sometimes experience political cohesion as a larger body politic, state and/or nation. However, individual human identification with the whole of the human species remains problematic for them, and is the primary condition that drives continuing tensions and conflicts of self-interest between individuals, communities, political groups, races, and/or nations. Humans must try to see the whole as one! *The survey will study whether humans can develop a means to remind themselves that they are part of a greater whole of human species so that they can become aware of a larger purpose to share the Earth sustainably for all humans.*

Flying south from Edinburgh to the next stop for the tour in Barcelona was a bit disorienting for Alvin. He had gotten used to the westerly direction of the tour's daytime flights oriented with the direction of Earth's rotation. The flight to Barcelona was from north to south, flying over the English coast, the Bay of Biscayne along the coast of France, then over the Pyrenees Mountains to the Mediterranean coast between France and Spain. It was a reminder for Alvin that the Earth is a three-dimensional sphere rotating on a north-south axis as it orbits around the Sun.

From the air, the jagged rocky expanse of the Pyrenees looked like the shards of a large ceramic jar smashed to bits. Latif told the tour group of the legend of Pyrene, a mythical princess after whom the Pyrenees was named.

"According to legend, she was the virginal daughter of Bebryx, a king in Mediterranean Gaul who shared his hospitality with the Greek hero Heracles during his quest to steal the cattle of Geryon in Erytheia. This was one of the famed twelve labors as foretold by the Oracle at Delphi that Heracles must do in penance for slaying his own sons when driven mad by the jealous queen of the gods Hera.

Heracles, drunk with his host's wine, repaid his host's hospitality by raping his daughter Pyrene. She became pregnant and gave birth to a serpent, before fleeing away to the woods where she was torn to pieces by wild beasts. After vanquishing the winged monster Geryon and sacrificing his cattle to Hera, Heracles passed through the kingdom of Bebryx again and came upon Pyrene's lacerated remains. In grief Heracles is said to have buried her remains by pushing together the surrounding mountains to form the Pyrenees.

Latif continued, "The Pyrene legend bears some metaphorical resemblance to geologic reality. According to paleontologic evidence, the Pyrenees were formed between a hundred to hundred fifty million years ago during the Lower Cretaceous period when the spreading plate movement of the Mid-Atlantic Rift Zone forced the present-day northeast corner of Spain against the lower southwest edge of France on the Eurasian continental plate. The intense pressure and uplifting due to the pushing together of the two land masses formed the Pyrenees.

"The Greek poet who authored the story of Heracles pushing the mountains together to form the Pyrenees must have been very discerning," Latif joked with the tour group, which was becoming used to his rambling but studious style of travel monologue.

"With a population of five million, Barcelona is the largest European city on the Mediterranean Sea and the second largest city in Spain after Madrid. Fronted by a wide and busy port, the city is located between the mouths of the Llobregat and Besos Rivers. To the west is Montserrat, the highest mountains of the Catalan coastal range. It is the site of the Benedictine Abbey de Montserrat, identified in Arthurian legend as the final location of the Holy Grail, and which became a pilgrimage site for its Black Virgin of Montserrat sanctuary.

"Barcelona was said to have been named after the Carthaginian general Hamilcar Barca, father of Hannibal, reputed to have founded the city on a military campaign from Carthage in the third century BCE. It was later taken over by the Romans who rebuilt it as a fortified town centered on the Mons Taber. The Roman layout can still be seen in the walled structures of the historical city center, the Barri Gotic. Fragments of former Roman walls were used to build subsequent structures, including the city's main cathedral, Basilica La Seu, founded in the fourth century CE. We will be staying at the Hotel Colon located right across the historic Plaza de la Catedral from the Basilica La Seu."

Upon arrival at the Hotel Colon, the tour group was surprised by its location in the historic center of Barcelona within walking distance of much of the city's historic attractions. The hotel had magnificent views of the city's main cathedral, and the plaza drew very colorful crowds all during the day. As the group was checking in, a large procession of about two hundred naked people on bicycles paraded through the plaza. Many were blowing horn *vuvuzelas* and wearing ornate hats and sunglasses, but otherwise had nothing else on. A majority was middle-aged, some with paunchy stomach rolls or cellulite-wrinkled thighs in a less than appetizing physical display, yet all seemed to be in a cheerful mood.

"What's going on? Is this a nudist parade?" Alvin asked the hotel doorman.

"No, *Señor*, it is a demonstration advocating for better bicycle lanes and safety laws. They are marching to City Hall on the Rambla Catalunya. They are naked only to attract your attention and make certain everyone within view gets their message. It is the way that we passionate Catalunyans do things here in Barcelona!"

He laughed heartily, and Alvin roared back in approval. Only two minutes after checking into the hotel, Alvin felt that he liked this city a lot already.

The next day the tour visited the Basilica de la Sagrada Familia, Church of the Holy Family, which was billed by Latif as one of the high points of the tour.

"When the city fathers made plans to construct a Catholic church on the east side of Barcelona in 1882, the Catalan architect Antoni Gaudi became involved and made it his labor of love for the remainder of his life. Gaudi applied modern engineering techniques and new structural materials to replicate natural forms for the structure with innovative and complex geometries. His design called for a central nave supported on parallel rows of tall, slender columns forming double main aisles, a peripheral ambulatory with seven apsidal chapels, and an outer structure of eighteen spires spaced around three main portals, each widely different in structure and ornamentation. At the time of his death in 1926, less than a quarter of the project was complete. The original sponsors had run out of funds, and due to the wishes of Gaudi's family members and the surviving foundation, continued construction is being funded only by private contributions and visitor donations. The construction reached a midpoint in 2010, and it is hoped that it will be completed by 2026, the centennial of Gaudi's death."

Taking a lift to the top, the tour began a walk down a long, spiraling walkway along the inner walls of the structure, stopping at many open balconies and apertures on all sides to view the exterior of the cathedral and the city of Barcelona along the way.

Back on the ground, the tour group viewed the exterior of the church and its three main portals with their grand façades: the Nativity façade to the east, the Passion façade to the west, and the Glory façade to the south.

Latif explained, "The Nativity façade was completed in 1930 and is dedicated to the birth of Jesus. Gaudi considered it the most hopeful and accessible of his symbolic designs and therefore the one that the public should see completed first. Facing the rising sun, a symbol for the birth of Christ, the façade is divided into three porticos carved with multitudes of human figures representing acts depicting the theological virtues of Hope, Faith and Charity.

"In contrast, the Passion façade is austere, with harsh straight lines that resemble a skeleton reduced to bone. The emaciated figure of Christ is depicted being scourged at the pillar, and dying in agony on the Cross. Gaudi wanted this façade to strike fear into the onlooker, showing the severity and brutality of Christ's sacrifice. It portrays people suffering in agony in Hell for their sins. Above the façade, the pyramidal pediment is made up of eighteen bone-shaped columns culminating in a large cross with a crown of thorns."

"The Glory façade was designed to be the largest and most striking, and would be the principal façade for access into the central nave. It is dedicated to the Celestial Glory of Jesus, representing the road to God through Death, Final Judgment, and Glory. Construction on the Glory façade started in 2002, making it the last that would be finished.

"The eighteen outer spires are for the twelve apostles, four evangelists, the Virgin Mary, and Jesus Christ. Eight spires for eight of the apostles have already been built. The central spire for Jesus Christ is to be surmounted by a giant cross reaching a total height of one hundred seventy meters, which was designed by Gaudi to be one meter less than the height of Barcelona's highest hill Montjuic, because he believed that his creation should not surpass God's. The completion of the Jesus Christ spire would make it the tallest church building in the world. The church is already in use, and in November 2010 Pope Benedict XVI came to consecrate the church, making it eligible to be recognized as a Roman Catholic cathedral."

Back inside the church, Latif took the tour group down the main aisle of the central nave and stood at the crossing with the transept.

"The central nave rises to forty-five meters in height, while the transverse naves are thirty meters high. The crossing rests on four central columns of porphyry supporting a great hyperboloid surrounded by two rings of twelve hyperboloids. The central vault rises to a height of sixty meters, and its apse is capped by a vault reaching seventy-five meters in height. Notice that these open troughs in the floor beneath the central apse allow you to see into the crypt below, bringing the living and the dead into communion as one."

After touring the church, Latif took the tour group to a nearby bistro for lunch. Sitting around a long table, the guests talked excitedly about the marvelous architectural work they had just seen.

"It is truly a work of art," said Jane. "The entire structure and all of its parts visually tell the complete story of Christianity."

"Yes, and with such emotion and feeling that it must reach everyone who sees it, no matter what race, religion or creed. It truly tells a story for all humanity," Ralph agreed.

"Why did it take so long for the Vatican to recognize it as a cathedral?" asked Mr. Tanaka.

"When it was first being constructed and when the details of Gaudi's elaborate depictions of the Passion of Christ became known, it was said that the Vatican thought it was heretical and refused to recognize it. Due to the reportage since Gaudi's death and the worldwide acclaim for this remarkable creation, I guess the Vatican could not ignore it any longer," replied Latif.

"That bodes well for the Vatican," said Iz. "Pope Benedict and Pope John Paul before him have held very regressive views of the Catholic Church's engagement with the world and even with Catholics. Especially in interfaith dialog, it seems that the Vatican has done little and offered little in reconciliation with other religions of the world and even with peoples other than traditional Catholics. Pope Benedict's consecration of Sagrada Familia seems to be at least a small sign of the Vatican's return to openness to the non-Catholic rest of humanity. Hopefully, this will be continued and expanded by the current Pope Francis."

"Well, you see how a work of art can perhaps change even the Vatican's mind," laughed Jane.

That evening the whole group went to dinner at *Les Quartre Gats*, a storied local restaurant within a short walk from the hotel toward the Plaza de Catalunya. The restaurant was a hangout for artists like Dali and Picasso before they became famous, and many artists paid for their meals with paintings that still hang on its walls. The main dining room was a large room painted bright yellow, with dark wood posts supporting a mezzanine gallery. A pianist and violinist played Catalan music, and the service was professional and prompt, with a minimum of tourism or snobbery.

Alvin sat next to Mr. Tanaka and Jane at a long table for the group, with Akiko and Iz sitting across. Everyone was in a festive mood, probably taking a cue from the naked bicycle parade. The tour guests were excited by the house menu which offered many Catalan specialties. Mr. Tanaka chose *"Arroz con Calamar Tinta Negro"* which he reported was cooked to perfection and very tasty. Closing her eyes and murmuring with delight, Jane tasted her *"Bacalao Catalan"* of salt cod cooked with Catalan spinach and honey aioli, in a mild tomato sauce garnished with preserved fruits. Alvin tried the *"Esquivar Mi-Cuit"* of duck with apple and Cumberland sauce, and was delighted by its soft texture and flavor. Akiko had the *"Puerco Iberico"* with apple raisin and raspberry sauce, which she said was very tasty and tender. Iz tried the *"Escalivada"* of baked bell pepper and aubergines simmered in a sauce of goat cheese, which he reported was lusciously soft and smooth. It was a memorable meal and ambiance to mark their stay in Barcelona.

On the way back to the hotel after dinner, Alvin walked with Iz and Akiko.

"We didn't see much of you the last days in Edinburgh," said Iz to Alvin.

"Yes, I stayed in to get started writing an article on a new scenario for nuclear arms control that came to me when we were in Istanbul," replied Alvin, giving Iz a long look.

"Oh, you mean the new angle that Al-Qaeda might recharge an old Soviet field nuclear weapon and use it to blast a Turkish air base and steal NATO nuclear weapons stored there? Well, that certainly seems like a scenario worth considering. Where are you planning to publish it?" asked Iz.

"I plan to submit it right away, so that by the time we get to New York City, I can discuss it with my former editor at *Arms Control Journal*. If they publish the article, I hope that it will forewarn arms control agencies to put in place procedures for monitoring terrorist actions to acquire and activate a field nuclear weapon," said Alvin. He wondered if Akiko was following the thread of his suspicions about Iz and his Islamic "friends" in Istanbul.

"Don't you think Al-Qaeda will also be warned to change what they are doing to avoid detection by those agencies? Wouldn't your article only warn them to make their movements more obscure and stealthy?" asked Iz with a serious look.

Alvin paused and had to admit that Iz had a good point. "Well, what else can we do?" he asked, saying "we" pointedly to include Akiko and especially Iz.

"Viewing the Sagrada Familia, I was reminded that our real 'holy family' is hope," replied Akiko, "the hope that humanity can surmount its life-threatening problems and thrive. Hope must extend even to one's enemies, as they are human too, and from their viewpoint, they are trying to do what seems right and just to them."

Iz seemed eager to reply to the question he had wanted Alvin to ask. "I believe that for arms control efforts to be effective in the wider context, it must also deal with how the nuclear-armed West is threatening those it perceives as enemies, especially Islamists. We in the West have the myopic view that we are the only ones doing good and are being fair and just to all. We are totally blind to how we threaten our perceived enemies. Such as by talk of a 'crusade' to topple Islamic governments and wipe Islamic radicals out. Such as by characterizing all Islamists who take up weapons to defend their interests as 'terrorists.' Such as by presenting our Christianity as the only good religion, and Islam as the evil one. How can we aspire to fostering hope for humanity when we promote such a one-sided view leaving out one-quarter of all humanity?"

Alvin was dumbstruck into silence. He had no answer, as he recognized that Iz was absolutely right.

Akiko picked up on Iz's thoughts. "All attempts at arms control directed at our perceived enemies, and especially Muslims, seem destined to fail because we cannot just eradicate our enemies, and they are simply not going to go away or accept an unjust position at the altar of humanity."

Alvin let these thoughts sink in. Finally, he said with a sigh, "You know, the funny thing is that we analysts like doing the hard stuff, like gathering intelligence on people, weapons, and communications.

But we seldom give thought to doing the human stuff, like cleaning up our divisive talk and reassuring others of our good intent. You're both right. I think I need to go back to work and write the other half of my article."

Iz grunted. Akiko gazed at Alvin with soft eyes, and a smile. Alvin felt like a wall between his divided selves had fallen. He felt whole, and good.

["Yes, try to see the whole as one!"]

Alvin spent the next day staying in his room reworking his article. The rest of the group toured the city, visiting the fortress and park on the heights of Montjuic, the museums, the Boqueria markets, and the shopping district of Eixample. At the end of the day, Alvin rejoined Iz and Akiko on the Ramblas for some relaxation over *cervezas* drinks and *pinchos* snacks.

"Well, how did your article work out," asked Iz with interest.

"Thanks to you and Akiko, I took a whole new perspective on the problem," Alvin replied. "We cannot just keep chasing down every jihadist who springs up. Even if we could catch every one and kill them, new ones, perhaps many more, will step forward. Instead, I tried to think about how we might address the larger problem, the fact that Islam has fundamental grievances with the West. Dr. Hans Kung once said, famously, 'There will be no peace among nations without peace among the religions.' So first off, the Islamic public needs reassurance that the West, especially Christianity, has good intentions toward Islam. The current Pope has reaffirmed his desire to re-engage reconciliation with other religions, as had been declared in the Vatican II Declaration of Gaudiam et Spes in nineteen sixty-five. My article suggests that perhaps the Vatican may be reminded of the importance of resuming interfaith dialog and that it may have a direct impact in weaning away Islamic public support of extremism.

"Second, how can we expect to deter nuclear proliferation by our enemies when we ourselves tolerate proliferation by our allies? A major reason for Islamic interest in acquiring nuclear weapons is the longstanding refusal of Israel to acknowledge that it maintains and deploys its own arsenal of nuclear weapons. Perhaps our President and the State Department may be reminded that the next global Review Conference for the Non-Proliferation Treaty has a nuclear-free Mideast on its agenda, and that a key State initiative has been to get Israel to sign the Non-Proliferation Treaty.

"Third, we know that a major risk for nuclear weapons proliferation in the future is increased use of nuclear power to keep pace with worldwide economic growth, and that the uranium fuel needed would contain enough fissionable byproducts to make ten times all the nuclear bombs that exist today. Perhaps the State Department may be reminded that the use of thorium as a nuclear fuel that does not generate fissionable material has long been proposed, and that the time is ripe to commission a feasibility study of conversion to thorium reactors for consideration in the next NPT Review.

"Finally, as part of reassuring the Islamic public, we should also remember that much of the Islamic public does not support extremism, and that many more will withdraw their support if they are reassured that the West is truly committed to a balance with their interests as well. How can the Islamic public be courted without interfering with their governments or their internal politics. Well, by the wonderfully open and free Internet! Perhaps non-proliferation websites can be set up in anticipation of the next NPT Review that would enable public citizens everywhere to participate in Review discussion forums. For the vast majority of citizens who do not support nuclear proliferation, they can post comments on such websites, including reports on any clandestine activities they may witness in their locales. This would get the whole world involved in working against nuclear proliferation at the ground level and make it more difficult for extremist groups to carry on clandestine activities."

Iz gave Alvin a broad smile. "That sounds truly enlightened, showing a higher level of consciousness for all humanity! I congratulate you! I could not have written better myself."

Akiko chimed in, "Alvin, that is truly wonderful. Let's hope it works."

The following day Alvin joined the group for a visit to the Abbey de Montserrat, about fifty kilometers west of Barcelona. Once off the highway, their bus kept climbing up the winding access road until breathing in the thinning air became noticeably harder. At over three thousand feet elevation, the bus finally pulled into a parking lot and let the guests out to visit the monastery grounds nestled among the crag walls of the towering mountain. They listened to *Escolania*, the Montserrat Boys' Choir famed throughout Europe, performing during mass in the basilica. They also rode the funicular up to Montserrat's highest point, from which they could see the wide expanse of the Catalonian coastal plain and the island of Majorca out at sea.

A long queue had formed to see the Santa Maria de Montserrat sanctuary in the rear of the basilica. Latif explained that the ebony wood statue of the Virgin Mary and infant Christ is referred to by its familiar Catalan name, *La Moreneta*, "little dark-skinned one." The statue is believed to be a Romanesque sculpture carved by local craftsmen from the twelfth century who were influenced by the Moorish culture in Spain. Legend has it that the Benedictine monks who came to construct the Abbey could not move the statue and instead built the Abbey around it. In 1881, Pope Leo XIII declared the Virgin of Montserrat the patroness saint of Catalonia.

When he finally reached the sanctuary, Alvin gazed intently at the statue, which was encased in protective glass, except for a gold ball extended on the Virgin's outstretched right hand. The front of the ball was accessible through an aperture in the glass. Alvin touched his fingers to the gold ball, and thought he felt a tingling sensation. Inspired, he said a silent prayer for peace and wellbeing of all people in the world.

"The reverence for Moreneta over a thousand years shows the true heart of Christians to respect all people of the world, doesn't it?" whispered Akiko behind him.

"Yes it does. It is inspiring that a simple sign of reverence by ordinary people can show that Christianity means well for all."

"I think that the article you are writing can have the same effect as you have included a commitment of goodwill towards the people of Islam," observed Akiko.

Alvin murmured his appreciation as he turned to look deep into Akiko's eyes.

> "From restless human mind came the will to create
> As well as to destroy, by unlocking dark secrets
> Of primal energy within the nucleus of matter
> To make weapons of mass death man's fate.
> Yet hope is our sacred family to nurture peace
> On Earth, through respect for all humanity,
> And grant us wisdom to cease our hostilities
> So man's better nature may become his destiny."

8

New York City: Ground Zero Revisited

[EXPLORATION LOG: EARTH CE, 74°W, 40°N, 06.22.2013, 12:30:01 PM]

As previously observed, humans are invested with the notion that their ultimate individual validation is the exercise of one's "free will." This can manifest in an individual continually voicing contrary opinions or doing the opposite of what another human commands or requests. By everyone acting contrarily to what anyone else may want, human actions can be ineffective in doing what common sense dictates would be best for all, a quality that I have called "human fecklessness."

However, probably as a survival skill, humans have also developed an opposite tendency that can get them to do implicitly what common sense dictates, which they recognize as "reverse psychology." So as not to denigrate their vaunted "free will," humans pretend that reverse psychology is something sneaky or clever and need not be voiced. A recent example was demonstrated in the empowerment of the women's liberation movement in the West by men suggesting that women needed to stay home for child-rearing, and women deciding by reverse psychology that they can "have it all" by going to work more effectively than men while still managing their families at home. On the other hand, men do not like to admit to reverse psychology but commonly apply it in sports, such as by redirecting the physical force of an opponent in martial arts, or tricking themselves into not using arm strength in golf by thinking about the rhythm of their swing instead. The survey will explore whether the skill of reverse psychology can get humans to act in their own best interests to survive the threat of nuclear arms proliferation.

The morning flight from Barcelona flew over Montserrat as it climbed to cruising altitude on its way to the tour's next destination New York City. Alvin could make out the stone buildings of the abbey perched among the rock cliffs they had visited the day before. The island of Majorca was visible on the horizon to the east. The plane continued to climb until Alvin could see the jagged mass of the Pyrenees passing below and the Picos Cantabria coming into view ahead. Soon the plane headed out over the Bay of Biscayne and the Atlantic Ocean. The tour was now on the home stretch headed back to the U.S. Latif and the tour guests settled in for a quiet, relaxing flight.

As the flight circled over the East River for its final approach into JFK airport under bright and clear skies, Alvin could see the Statue of Liberty with her upheld torch on the pedestal island at the confluence of the East River with the Hudson River. He murmured to himself, "Our country still holds out the light of the world." Then he saw the bulge called the Battery at the foot of Manhattan island, and searched for the gaping hole among the tall buildings where the World Trade Center twin towers used to be. This was called "Ground Zero" after both towers were destroyed by planes crashed into them by Al-Qaeda terrorists, taking three thousand people to their deaths in a massive pile of twisted metal and debris. Scanning a ten-mile radius around that point, Alvin could imagine how Ground Zero would look if the planes had carried a hijacked nuclear weapon.

The tour group checked into a midtown Manhattan hotel, and had free time in the afternoon for sightseeing at nearby points of interest. Alvin went to see his former editor David Kendall at the midtown office of the *Arms Control Journal*.

"Hi, David, so good to see you. Gosh, you don't look a day older since I left Manhattan fifteen years ago!"

"Oh, you were always good to me, Al. A man my age always appreciates being thought of as a decade or two younger. How has life in Hawaii been treating you? I heard that your work at East-West Institute has been focusing on clandestine nuclear weapons proliferation."

"Yes, Hawaii is not such a backwater you know. We have quite a few expat members of the Pahlevi family living there, as well as some recent Mideast emigrés. It's always amazing what you might hear over a round of golf or after-work *pau hana* hour," laughed Alvin.

"Well, thanks for sending me your article to review. It's excellent work! We have already sent it to press to be published the day after tomorrow in the next Journal issue. I especially liked your suggested framework of balancing military deterrence of a new strategic threat of terrorist action with needed social interventions to reduce tensions between the Islamic public and the West," said David appreciatively.

"A little birdie, or two, gave me a tweet. Thanks, David. I'm thrilled to have the Journal publish it."

"There is no question that this is entirely timely and appropriate," said David. "I've been thinking how we can get the publication read by the powers-that-be so that they might act on it. As for deterring field nuclear weapon reactivation, I would like to send the article to my friend the UN Ambassador Delegate. As you know, she is the State Department's Special Representative for the President on Nuclear Non-Proliferation. She probably already has it on her agenda to put tritium recharge scenarios on the IAEA watch lists.

"Regarding promoting Christian reconciliation with Islam, I think the Most Reverend Henry Holland, Bishop of Chicago, is our man. He is Chairman of the Committee on International Justice and Peace, U.S. Conference of Catholic Bishops. He has been active in reviewing the Church's position against nuclear weapons proliferation and briefs the Vatican on these issues. He would understand the importance for the Vatican to make progress on defusing tensions for Christianity with Islam.

"As for getting Israel to sign the NPT, the U.S. position was changed after the last Review to suggest that it was timely for Israel to do so, and of course Israel stonewalled any such suggestion. But even Israel's top generals now recognize that provoking a wider Mideast war by bombing Iran's nuclear facilities is not a working option. Other Islamic countries will be pressing to develop or acquire nuclear weapons unless the situation is de-escalated by Israel coming clean and committing to the NPT. Israel wants to get advanced anti-missile defense technology from the U.S., and it can negotiate a transfer in exchange for signing the NPT. The U.S. will get political cover from Islamic opposition to advanced anti-missile defense transfer if Israel does so. So it is timely for this suggestion to go back on State's agenda for the next Review.

"As for commissioning a thorium reactor feasibility study, that suggestion was of course made almost fifty years ago when the NPT was first being drafted. But the difference now is that the nuclear-armed powers have all the weapons-grade material they can use, and instead the threat of clandestine proliferation will be greatly multiplied if uranium fuel continues to be used in expanding numbers of power reactors for economic growth. I will send your article to Commissioner Davis at the NPT Secretariat, with a reminder that even the nuclear power industry association has been asking for a thorium study since Fukushima.

"Finally, your suggestion for public NPT Review websites and a 'Tweet Network' for citizen monitoring of clandestine proliferation activities is a no-brainer! I will put it before our Journal board right away for resources to set up a public website on the upcoming Review Conference and especially the Middle East Nuclear-Free Zone agenda. That one's easy!" David laughed with a wink.

"You're the best, David," Alvin said in appreciation.

David nodded emphatically with a smile. "You've put the right package together at the right time, Al. We should never have let you move to Hawaii. The NPT would be years ahead by now."

David's voice dropped, and his tone turned serious. "Al, I have to ask you. All this terrorists-after-nukes stuff is well and good in theory, but what support do you have that the threat might be real? Do you have any evidence that a terrorist group may be trying to acquire or activate a nuclear weapon?"

Alvin was silent for a long minute. Then he said, "David, if I show you some photographic evidence, can you guarantee me that any innocent persons involved will not be harmed?"

"You know I can't guarantee that," replied David. "But you have my promise that I will try to maintain confidentiality to the maximum extent possible."

Alvin pulled his digital camera out of his pocket, turned on the viewer, and stopped at the photos of Iz meeting with the three Islamic-looking men in the restaurant in Istanbul. "This person on the right is Isfahan Ghazen, a naturalized U.S. citizen from Egypt originally. He did his doctorate work in quantum physics with Peter Higgs at University of Edinburgh, before taking a job with a computer company in the Bay Area called MicroSimulation Systems. He said that his work is on contract with Livermore Labs to do simulation research on advanced nuclear weapons design. Notice the classified document seal on the folder he is turning over to the two men sitting on the left."

David looked carefully at the photos in the viewer display. "In this one, the man in the center with the stone face looks familiar from State Department internal reports I've seen, but I don't recall offhand. The other two I don't recognize. I'll have my State Department contact run a check and get back to you. Can you leave the flash memory with me?"

"Yes," Alvin said. He thought about the implications of State Department involvement, but was relieved to put this information in the hands of his old friend who would know how to check it out.

"OK, now our work is done," said David. "Let's get some lunch. My treat at Wolfie's Deli!"

The next day was a free day for the tour guests. Alvin, Akiko and Iz went to the Museum of Modern Art and were delighted to see a visiting exhibition of the paintings of the Mexican artist Frida Kahlo. The Overtons and Hadleys took a walking tour around Rockefeller Center. Jane and Ralph were ecstatic to get tickets for a matinee recital at Carnegie Hall. Mr. Tanaka and Lee were also lucky to find a visiting exhibition of Buddhist paintings from the Tang Dynasty at the Asia House Gallery. Latif as usual was busy making arrangements for the next days' tours.

At the end of a full day, the tour group had a special dinner reserved at the Four Seasons Restaurant in midtown. The restaurant's menu had just been changed and featured seasonal game meats, mushrooms and organic vegetables and herbs. The wine list included some well-known California vintages that had just made the "ready to drink" list. The guests marveled at the restaurant's high-ceilinged interior designed by architects Mies van der Rohe and Philip Johnson, and paintings by famous Expressionist artists. The whole effect was an exquisite marriage of modernism and money. Afterwards the tour guests walked back to the hotel along Park Avenue, enjoying the early summer night's air.

The next day the tour group went to visit the September 11 Memorial at Ground Zero. It felt eerie to Alvin to wander among the rows of tall trees surrounding the two large square pools where the Twin Towers once stood. He had lived in Manhattan since the time the towers were first built, and still could not get used to seeing the Lower Manhattan skyline without them. The falling leaves from the park's trees swirling down in the wind reminded Alvin of the televised coverage of the towers burning and the bodies of people falling to the ground as they chose to jump to their deaths rather than roast alive in the inferno.

"It's hard to imagine that those twin towers were actually here and are now completely gone," Iz said to Alvin as they walked the site.

"Every time I think about it, the images of the planes crashing into the towers and the scenes of resulting chaos seem to recede just a bit further from my mind," said Alvin.

"Perhaps our minds need to have a way of forgetting such horrific events," replied Iz.

"Well, that is why we have memorials, I suppose," said Alvin.

"The great thing about this Memorial is that it celebrates the life that comes after tragedy," Iz observed.

Alvin wondered, "Do we always need to suffer a tragedy before we will choose life?"

That afternoon the tour group was on free time. Most of the tour guests chose to visit the Metropolitan Museum of Art, but Alvin decided to skip it. The sudden release of finishing the rewrite of his article and getting it published removed a huge burden from him. He opted to go to the hotel spa for a sauna and deep tissue massage, followed by a long nap. "The pleasures of peace," he thought happily.

Later the tour guests gathered in the hotel lobby for another dinner out.

Alvin came down and joined the group. "Aren't we missing Iz?" he asked.

Just then Latif came rushing to the group from the elevator. "Something bizarre has happened to Iz. He was arrested this afternoon by the FBI. The hotel staff manager was ordered to open his door and heard the FBI agents tell Iz he was under arrest on charges of espionage. I tried to contact the FBI office in New York, but they claim not to have any knowledge of the arrest. We are trying to get more information through the police department."

Latif's face was ashen with worry. "This has never happened before. Please, everyone, try to stay calm. Go on ahead to dinner. I will stay at the hotel and try to contact the authorities to find out what happened."

Alvin went with the others to dinner, but he had no appetite thinking about Iz's arrest. While they ordered, he decided to try calling David's office late to see if the arrest had anything to do with the photos of Iz's meeting in Istanbul that he turned over.

"Oh, hi David. I'm glad you're still at the office. Our tour guest Isfahan Ghazen was arrested this afternoon by the FBI at our hotel, allegedly for spying against the U.S. Do you know anything about it?"

David replied after a long silence. "I'm sorry, Al. I wanted to tell you first, but the FBI said I could not. They did not want Mr. Ghazen warned in any way. Our State Department check of your photos confirmed that the stone-faced guy is Abu Al-Rashid, a reputed contact for Al-Qaeda in Turkey."

Alvin was stunned, and did not know what to say.

After another long silence, David offered, "You may get a call from a Jeff Peterson from State's bureau in New York City who will be handling the investigation. They will want to interview you, your tour guide Latif Yousef, and the other tour guests to get whatever information they can on Mr. Ghazen. I'm very sorry about this, Al. The news reports may say that some tour photos confirmed the meeting of Mr. Ghazen with a known terrorist leader, but your name will not be mentioned. They could have come from anyone's camera. Meanwhile, I'll keep you posted on your article's publication. Be well, and call me anytime you need to."

Alvin hung up. He tried to absorb the implications of Iz's arrest. When he went back to the dining table, he did not say anything to the others. It was better that they hear from Latif whatever details he was given. Alvin knew the State Department would not disclose what evidence they had. They would only question the tour guests for whatever information they could give them about Iz. Later, Alvin could not recall what he even had for dinner.

9
San Francisco: Home Is Where the Heart Is

[EXPLORATION LOG: EARTH CE, 123°W, 37°N, 06.26.2013, 2:00:01 PM]

Despite any childhood grievances, most humans remember their family home environment and growing up in their communities as the time in their lives when they felt safest, cared for and at peace. As they grow to young adults in pursuit of vocations and professions, they typically move from their hometowns to other locations, often never to return. Yet the memory of peace in their home environment remains with them for their entire lives, and is the benchmark by which they may gauge their subsequent life's experiences. This persistence of memory of home can enable humans to feel at peace wherever their location on Earth, and, if they consciously choose, could enable them to access a higher consciousness of the whole Earth as their home.

The key to humans acting to avoid nuclear weapons proliferation and other threats to their survival on Earth is to access their higher consciousness to see life on Earth as a whole and to experience being at one with the life-affirming spirit of the Universe. They must try to see the whole as one! *The study will conclude with a survey whether the persistence of memory of home can enable humans to access their higher consciousness and take the steps necessary for their survival.*

The tour group stayed sequestered at their hotel their last day in New York City while they were being interviewed by federal authorities in the investigation of spying charges against Iz. Alvin had to wall off his mind from anything that might refer to the photos he took of Iz in Istanbul. He had to take care of what he said to Akiko as well. He felt that she sensed his distancing himself from her and the others, but she remained warm towards him and did not ask him about it.

The morning they left New York for San Francisco, the last destination on the tour, their flight flew west on a clear day over the breadth of continental United States. Latif pointed out features below as the diversity of landscapes unfolded between East and West Coasts. The dense concrete highways and clusters of industrial areas of the New York metropolitan area soon gave way to a green patchwork of Pennsylvania farms carved out among rills of hilly forests. As the plane flew further west over Ohio, the eastern Allegheny and Appalachian plateaus flattened out into a puzzleblock terrain of farm lands bordered by Lake Erie to the north. The expanse of fertile farmlands continued over Indiana and into Illinois, the boundaries of which were marked by the Wabash River meandering south from Lake Michigan. Soon the urban expanse of the Chicago metropolitan region was visible to the north on the shores of Lake Michigan.

The Mississippi River marked the western border of Illinois with Iowa and Missouri, which historically has defined the divide between eastern and western halves of the United States down to the Gulf of Mexico. West of the Mississippi River past the farmlands of Iowa stretched a vast expanse of fertile grasslands known as the Great Plains. Explorers on the Lewis and Clark expedition in 1805 reported that one could stand from any vantage point and see tall grass stretching in every direction to the horizon. Great herds of buffalo once foraged on the Great Plains, and tribes of Indians numbering in the millions lived on its plentiful resources.

From the air, Kansas appeared as a flat expanse of farmlands bordered by the Missouri River to the northwest and stretching hundreds of miles to the high plains of Colorado. Nestled in the expanse leading to the foothills of the Rockies was the Denver and Fort Collins metropolitan area. Further west the Rockies appeared as a towering range of high peaks marking the continental divide of the U.S. Waters draining west of the continental divide flowed west into the Colorado River and eventually into the Gulf of California, while waters draining east of the divide flowed into the Missouri and Platte Rivers to the Mississippi River and eventually the Gulf of Mexico.

West of the Rockies, the plane flew over the Wasatch Mountain range in the north of Utah to its western side tapering down the valleys of central Utah. The urban area of Salt Lake City came into view on the shores of the Great Salt Lake. Further west the Great Basin appeared as a vast depression that was once an inland sea and is now an arid desert extending from the Great Salt Lake in Utah to the Mojave Desert in lower California at its southwestern end. Further west the Sierra Nevada range extended down the western side of Nevada into California. Past the Sierra Nevadas, Alvin could see the broad Central Valley stretching north to south across the upper half of California where one-third of the nation's food is grown. Finally reaching California's western coast, Alvin could see the metropolitan expanse of San Francisco spread across the Bay Area to the shores of the Pacific Ocean.

As the plane flew over East Bay into San Francisco airport, Alvin felt like he was coming home. Even though he had worked most of his career on the East Coast and now resided in Hawaii, he remembered growing up and going to college and law school in the Bay Area long afterwards. He recalled that his first lover, whom he met at a college mixer, was also from the Bay Area and had been his first experience of love. He remembered his favorite law professor at Berkeley and how he had let out a great belly laugh in class when Alvin, reading a law case title, mispronounced "La Jolla" with a hard "J" and "L" instead of with soft sounds as "la hoya." He also remembered the grand time he had hiking with his Bay Area friends around Mount Tamalpais, getting high on pot and seeing the hippies living in the forests making love *au naturel*. These and other memories always gave Alvin the feeling he associated with San Francisco of people being their natural selves and feeling "at home."

The tour group checked into the Palace Hotel, a landmark on Market and Montgomery Streets, and had an early dinner in its famed Garden Court atrium. The setting sun lit up the grand stained glass dome spanning the vast atrium with a fiery gold light. In the warmth of that glow, the tour guests enjoyed a delightful sampling of contemporary American dishes and storied California wines of recent vintage.

The next morning Alvin was surprised to receive a phone call to his room after breakfast.

"Hi, Alvin, guess who?"

"Iz, is that you? How the heck are you able to call me? Did the FBI release you?"

"No, nothing as easy as that. I called to thank you."

"Thank me? Why? It was my photos of you in Istanbul that got you into trouble!"

"That's what I called to explain, to set your heart at ease. Everything I say now is in absolute confidence, only for you to hear, OK? You were supposed to photograph me meeting with those Al-Qaeda contacts, to provide supporting evidence in the resulting investigation that a leak of classified material for nuclear weapons diversion may have occurred."

"What? I don't get it," said Alvin totally puzzled. "You mean I was set up to be present in the restaurant to photograph you? How did you set me up? I didn't even know you were going to be there."

"Well, let's just say that Akiko is in on the sting too," laughed Iz. "Remember, she suggested you bring your camera, chose the restaurant, and picked the table behind the potted plants. Then she left to go to the ladies room, and left you alone after pointing me out meeting with the other men. What can we expect an arms control analyst with a camera hidden behind potted plants to do after viewing a U.S. nuclear scientist hand a State Department folio for classified material to some shady looking characters?"

"But why are you doing this? Why did you want to be caught?" asked Alvin, thoroughly confused now.

Iz gave a thoughtful sigh. "Let's just say I was recruited by the State Department to be the pigeon to give classified weapons information to Al-Qaeda, given my Egyptian background, training in nuclear physics, and classified work on nuclear weapons design for a U.S. research lab. To convince Al-Qaeda that the information was credible, I had to be arrested when another passenger happened to photograph me with my contacts. That passenger also happened to be an arms control analyst who was alarmed enough to write an article on the scenario of field nuclear weapon recharge by Al-Qaeda. The ensuing media uproar over endangerment to the West would only make Al-Qaeda more determined to capitalize on the tritium recharge information. But the information is bogus, and would lead to their unwitting discharge of a rare isotope that can be traced by special sensors when my prescribed tritium recharge is attempted."

"How did you know I was going to be on the tour?" asked Alvin.

"No, it's the other way around. The State Department picked the tour for me and Akiko to go on when their research found that you would be on the tour. An article written by a respected analyst like you and the leak of confirming photos were essential for the sting to work and have credibility to both sides."

"So what happens to you now?" asked Alvin. "You are a marked man, by both sides."

"It was prearranged. This was a very important sting operation by CIA to divert Al-Qaeda's nuclear ambitions. The FBI will announce that I have agreed to cooperate with Federal authorities and take a plea agreement. Supposedly, I will get fifteen years in a Federal maximum-security prison. Instead, my family and I will get new identities in the State Department's witness protection program.

We will be well taken care of. I will even have a new job working in a classified government lab. My family discussed it fully beforehand. We decided that it was an important action, that it was our duty in repayment of the privilege we have had to be U.S. citizens, and it was also what we could do to help prevent or slow the Middle East from going down the road to nuclear proliferation. My daughter likes acting anyway, so for her it is like being in an exciting new play."

"Iz, I don't know how to say this, but I have always felt a special place for you, even as I was being led to suspect your activities. You seem to understand the big picture and have a big heart for all despite being Muslim."

In his best rendition of ebonics, Iz intoned, "Ah love yah too, bro. Gimme a huggg!" Iz laughed. "I'll stay in touch, I promise. State will know how I can reach you. Oh, and congratulations on having your article being published in *Arms Control Journal*. You'll have to go on the talk circuit now. And please give Akiko my love, you devil you!"

Iz hung up. Alvin laughed aloud in his room. Then he pulled open his room window and shouted to the skies his thanks to God.

After a day of touring, Latif and the guests planned to go for dinner at Fisherman's Wharf to celebrate the end of their around-the-world tour of historic places. This would be their last evening together before all were to depart for home. Latif, Mr. Tanaka, Lee and Alvin got together beforehand for drinks at the Pied Piper Bar downstairs in the hotel. They sat at the long bar over which hung the original Maxfield Parrish mural of "The Pied Piper of Hamlin."

"Well, this has been a wonderful trip," said Mr. Tanaka. "We have all enjoyed visiting these special places around the Earth, and thanks to Latif, and to Alvin and Iz also, we learned so much about the histories and stories of these places."

"Indeed, I have learned so much from all of you too," said Latif.

"We all learned from each other. Mr. Tanaka really opened my eyes to Japan and the Japanese people, and Lee did the same for China," Alvin said.

"I learned most of all how important it is to do what we can about our problems in the present, rather than creating even greater problems for the next generation," replied Lee.

"Speaking of which, it is shocking that Iz was arrested for spying for terrorists, while at the same time, Alvin's article on reducing tensions between Islam and the West has been very well received in the news," said Mr. Tanaka.

"No, I don't think Iz was spying for terrorists," Alvin said hopefully. "He seemed to be a standup guy to me. Maybe it was all a misunderstanding whether materials from his work were classified or not. Anyway, let's hope for the best."

"Since we are sitting in front of this artwork, have you heard the story of the Pied Piper?" Lee asked tentatively. He remembered the horrified looks from the tour guests the last time he told a story.

"Yes, it is something about a magician who lured all the children out of a village with pipe music, isn't it?" asked Mr. Tanaka.

"Well, the way it was told to me by a history teacher in school, there is a bit more to the real story," Lee started. "It seems that there was a very wealthy town in the Middle Ages called Hamlin in Germany. The town had a rat infestation, but could not get rid of them. One day an itinerant man dressed in pied clothing appeared, claiming to be a rat-catcher who could solve their problem. The mayor promised that the town would pay him to get rid of the rats, and the man accepted. He pulled out a musical pipe and used a special tune to lure the rats out of town to drown in a nearby river. However, the mayor grew arrogant and refused to pay the man what was promised. The man left the town angrily, but vowed revenge. One Sunday while the townspeople were all in church, the man appeared and played his pipe again, this time with a tune to lure the young children of Hamlin. The children followed the piper out of town thinking it was a game. In some versions of the story, the children all drowned. In others, they were taken away and never seen again. The moral of the story is that we must do what we are responsible for now, otherwise our children will pay the price."

"Amen to that," Alvin agreed.

"Hi guys," Akiko greeted them as she came down to join the

group for dinner. "Oh, and congratulations, Alvin! I read a rave review of your article in the Huffington Post. It said that it was a very timely exposé combined with a holistic approach to reducing tensions between the West and Islamic countries that made great sense."

"Well, thank you," said Alvin. "I took my inspiration from all of your thoughtful insights on this trip."

Later, as he and Akiko took a taxi together from the hotel to the restaurant, Alvin asked the question that had been bothering him. "Akiko, you are a puzzle to me. Why did you help in the CIA sting after the treatment you got from the U.S. government when your husband died?"

Akiko blushed. "Oh, you mean my role in stringing you along with my allure? Honestly, I got involved on a whim," she laughed. "The subject came up indirectly in settlement discussions with government negotiators on my long-unresolved wrongful death claim. They said they could justify a more generous settlement if I were willing to do something useful for the government in return. I asked what, and they said that the CIA might have need of an attractive female who liked to travel to distract a male passenger present to witness a clandestine meeting while touring in a foreign city. I thought, hmm, that sounds extremely unlikely to happen and exciting at the same time, so I agreed to make myself available. It was only when they came back with the scenario for this around-the-world tour that I realized they were serious. But I felt it would be a good way to honor the work my husband did by doing what I could to help the United States."

She added, "However, when I got to know you, the job turned out to be more difficult emotionally than I had expected."

Alvin gave Akiko a big hug and was silent a long while.

"Shall we remain friends even after the trip, and the 'job' ends?" quipped Alvin.

"Of course we shall. I will come to Hawaii at some point and meet your family. Perhaps by then we can tell them about our double-oh-seven escapade!" she said, tearing a bit.

"I will look forward to that very much," said Alvin.

"To love renewed!" whispered Akiko, with a kiss.

Epilogue:
The Song Will Go On

"Catastrophe or temperate life, is one needed
To have the other, or can man choose the better?
Man by free will can refuse what good sense tells,
But can learn to bring about the good by nurture.
A choice starts with the first moment of awareness,
Then the first step taken follows with the next, no less.
This is the way the Spirit can attain that which is best:
Taking the right step now, so that good may manifest."

[Exploration Log: Earth CE, 158°W,
21°N, 06.30.2013, 2:00:01 PM]

Humans on Planet Earth have a long history of fomenting death and destruction on each other, but somehow each worse catastrophe of their own doing seems to make their resolve to survive stronger. But when tragedy ends and peace again reigns, they gradually forget how it happened. Free will allows them to choose a path sometimes opposite to what good sense requires, but reverse psychology may get them to act wisely when they realize that the fate of all humans and their succeeding generations is at stake. Their accessing of a higher consciousness for all humanity may allow humans a chance to overcome their propensity toward nuclear weapons proliferation and other global threats to their survival. The outcome is as yet unknown, and requires further monitoring.

With Alvin's return from his world tour to Hawaii, my travels on Earth have come to an end for now. I will schedule in the log a follow-up study of human probability of survival on Earth to be conducted in five years time. Over and out.

Acknowledgments

I would like to thank Dr. Patrick Takahashi, retired professor of biochemistry and analyst on energy policy turned world traveler and bon vivant, for the inspiration to try writing a book of fiction from a scientific perspective. I hope this book will be read by readers young and old with a sense of wonder at the miraculous world that is knowable through mankind's remarkable scientific achievements.

I would like to acknowledge the inestimable resources of world knowledge made available through Wikipedia, the global online and free encyclopedia created by Jimmy Wales, Larry Sanger, Tim Shell, Jason Richey, and some twenty-two thousand contributors to Wikipedia's four million articles in English. Equal acknowledgement is due to Google, the global online and free search engine created by Larry Page, Sergei Brin, Terry Winograd and many others participating in Google's grand experiment to make all of the world's knowledge searchable online. The Wikipedia and Google tools enabled me to research and confirm topical subjects in almost any field instantaneously from my desk, greatly assisting my writing this work of science-based fiction.

My heartfelt thanks to my editor Gail Honda of Global Optima who took on the unenviable task of editing a manuscript that was walled in by dense, pages-long expositions of scientific and historical facts and making it a joy to read.

I also want to thank Benedict Palmieri, a man wise in the ways of human nature with a great sense of humor, who told me the joke about aliens discovering that humans had nuclear weapons that provided the inspiration for me to write this book.